MW00879115

Bad Boy Rock Star

Bad Boy Rock Star, Volume 1

Candy J Starr

Published by Candy J Starr, 2014.

BAD BOY ROCK STAR

First edition. May 19, 2014.

Copyright © 2014 Candy J Starr.

Written by Candy J Starr.

Also by Candy J Starr

Access All Areas
Too Many Rock Stars

Bad Boy Rock Star
Bad Boy Rock Star
Bad Boy vs Millionaire
Bad Boy Redemption
Angie: A Short Story from the Bad Boy Rock Star Series
Bad Boy Rock Star: The Complete Story

Fallen Star
Rock You
Cry for You
Be With You

Standalone
Hands Off! The 100 Day Agreement

Watch for more at candyjstarr.com.

Chapter 1

He kissed me and he changed my world forever, although I never would have dreamt it at the time. It was just a kiss, not even a particularly passionate kiss at that. But, in all my twenty-two years, I'd never been kissed so annoyingly, so teasingly, so spine-tinglingly arrogantly.

I hated Jack Colt.

He'd grabbed me and pressed his lips against mine as if to say, "I could give you so very much more but I *choose* not to." Like, if he wanted, he could unleash a power that would annihilate my world and sweep away everything that had gone before him. The force of him could wrap my heart, squeeze it tight and draw out every desire, even the ones I kept hidden from myself.

He was an unstoppable force.

I tried to ignore the sparks tingling my skin where he touched me. His hand on the back of my neck, his fingers tangled in my hair. Bolts of pure electricity ran through me, making my toes curl and my back arch. My hands struggled at my sides, wanting to feel his skin and pull his face closer to mine. I splayed my fingers to control myself.

Even that wasn't enough. My lips moved with his and my body leaned against him. I don't know why. I didn't want him kissing me. I didn't want his flesh against mine.

I could've pulled away. Could've. Should've. But I didn't.

The soft leather of his thigh pressed between my legs and I pressed back without thinking. I was drowning and I wasn't sure if I liked it but I wanted more.

Then he stopped.

I pushed him away, willing my knees not to buckle and my legs not to shake. I was in control. I'm always in control. I'm the girl that everyone wants to make happy. I'm the girl that guys fall in love with at first sight, then follow around, making complete idiots of themselves in the hopes that maybe, for a brief instant, I'll notice they existed. I definitely don't lose control of myself because some thug forces his lips on mine.

But he'd not even given me a chance to say no.

I wanted to slap his face for daring to pounce on me like that but I also needed to keep my cool. I took a deep breath to calm myself and brushed myself down, brushing every bit of him off me. I could handle this situation.

Then I gave him my best bitch look.

Jack Colt, the kind of man I most despise. That slow, lazy arrogance, the black hair tumbling down into his deep brown eyes. Eyes that mocked me with a look that said he could take what he wanted from me any time. The sleazy five o'clock shadow.

He wasn't even that good-looking; he just reeked of animal masculinity with an energy he could barely contain. It burst out of him like the biceps bursting out of his t-shirt sleeves and the muscles straining out of the tight leather pants and the... I wasn't even going to look at that.

People like me don't even acknowledge the existence of people like him. He was the kind of people that washed my Mercedes or worked in the garden. Not the kind of person who thrusts their tongue between my carefully painted lips.

"Like that, princess?" He spat out the word *princess* like it was an insult but I'd always been a princess. I took it as a compliment.

"I-I-I..."

Why couldn't I string a basic sentence together? What happened to my carefully prepared speech? I had to be tougher than anyone, that's what my dad said. You can be a princess but you have to be tough.

"You can buy CDs out the front if you want one signed."

He nodded at the table set up in the other room, then grabbed the green-haired girl beside me. The girl I'd known for all of two minutes and already hated. Now his lips locked onto hers while she balanced on tiptoes in those platform boots to reach him.

What the hell was this guy thinking? Why would I want his autograph? Heat rose through my face as it dawned on me what he'd meant. He thought I was some desperado groupie looking for a cheap grope like the rest of these skanks waiting in line. I'd make him regret that mistake. I'd come here on business, business I needed to discuss right now. I most definitely wasn't here for him to play stupid kissing games with his lips of death.

I'd arrived at the bar about a half hour earlier, expecting there to be some kind of office or room where we could speak in private.

"The band room's at the back," the girl on the door had said. "But you still have to pay the cover charge if you aren't on the list."

How could I be on a list? If I'd known any other way to contact the band, I wouldn't have come here at all. This place reeked of stale beer and cheap cologne.

I'd pushed my way through the mass of people, most of them sweaty and gross and drunk enough to be annoying.

A horrible grating sound came from the stage and I assumed that was them. Storm. No matter. I didn't have to like their music. The man at the front, Jack Colt, strutted around the stage like some kind of fancy man and the way he touched that guitar, it bordered on obscene. How could these people watch that? It was like looking through someone's bedroom window and catching them in an act of disturbing intimacy.

And how did carpet get so sticky and gross? Didn't these people ever clean? As I noticed a guy stumble from the bar trying to balance four beers in his hands, that question was answered.

He tottered near me and spilt some of it on my shoes. My very fabulous, very expensive shoes.

"What the hell do you think you are doing?" I yelled at him but my voice got lost in the screech of guitar from onstage and the idiot merged back into the crowd.

Someone shoved me in the back and cold liquid touched my skin. Then someone trod on my foot and didn't even apologise. I tried to push through the crowd but most of them just pushed me back. Elbows pierced my side, whole bodies slammed into me.

And seriously, couldn't they turn the music down a bit? The world must be full of deaf people if they listened to this music. I'd been to concerts before but they were nothing like this. This was a hundred or so people packed into a tiny room that pretty much resembled Hell.

I could see the doorway leading to the back of the stage. I kept my eyes on it and tried to move in that direction.

Another foot thumped onto mine so I thumped back, making good use of my stiletto heels.

Then, without any apparent reason apart from some herd mentality, they all surged forward, trying to squeeze into the already crowded space. A can flew out of nowhere and bashed me on the head. It stung like hell and might have even cut me.

I wanted to flee from this room to a place where sweat and beer didn't exist but I needed to talk to that man.

As the crowd surged further forward, I slipped around the back of them.

I finally got to the band room, well, the space outside the band room, sort of at the back of the stage. An area full of black cases and boxes with "Marshall" written on them. Who was Marshall and why did he get personalised boxes? To the right, large doors led outside. To the other side was a graffiti-covered door that I assumed was the band room.

I tried to get to the back room to wait for the band to come offstage, but a huge guy with his arms folded and a "don't mess with me" look on his face blocked my way. He stood in front of the door as though guarding something valuable.

"I'm here to talk to the band." I put on my best bitchface and squared up to him but it just ricocheted right off.

"Are you on the list?"

"Look at me. Do I look like I'm not important?"

He glanced over my outfit, then grunted.

"Hard to know. Chicks do all kinds of shit to get in the back room."

"Well, I don't. I have a meeting. A business meeting."

"Maybe you do, but I wasn't told about it. Wait over there with the rest of 'em." He nodded his head at a group of five girls.

"But you don't understand—"

"Either wait there or get out!"

That didn't give me a lot of choice. Then a woman in leather pants and long black hair breezed past the bouncer.

"How come she's allowed—"

The big guy snarled and pointed at the exit. He'd be sorry when he found out who I was. Then he'd apologise because I had more right to access that room than any chick in leather pants. I held my Vuitton bag tight by my side, hoping none of these drunken people had bad intentions, and huddled as close to the door as I could.

One girl said hello but I ignored her. I could barely hear her over that insane noise onstage anyway.

Then the band went quiet and the crowd screamed. I smoothed down my skirt, getting ready to corner them as they came offstage. That's when the green-haired girl sprang out from nowhere. She stopped abruptly when she saw me, giving my outfit the up and down, then sniggered.

A guy with his head shaved pushed through the girls, the bouncer holding the door open for him.

"Hey, Spud," one of the girls called.

He raised his eyebrows in response.

"Jack'll be here soon," he said.

The girl made a weird whimper.

"If you bitches really cared, you'd have been out front watching the band instead of hanging around here," the green-haired girl snorted.

Then she turned to me. Her gaze started at my feet and worked its way up in silent judgement. I could play that game too. In fact, when it came to *that* game, I could win Olympic gold.

My shoes were designer high heels probably ruined from this disgusting carpet; hers were huge platform boots covered with straps and buckles like some kind of straitjacket for your feet.

Silk stockings caressed my long, shapely legs. The flesh of her stumpy legs squeezed out through the rips in her fishnets.

My skirt had been a pivotal part of this season's fashion collections. Her skirt was some red plaid thing that screamed second-hand.

Her t-shirt barely contained her ample flesh. Me – elegance and sophistication with a touch of cheeky fun.

She dangled some kind of furry red backpack from her arm. My bag had featured in this month's *Vogue*, although the designer had offered it to me months ago. Part of the VIP service.

She had a turned-up nose covered in freckles. I had the best nose money could buy.

Her eyes were ringed in black eyeliner, making her look like a panda. My nude make-up accentuated my sapphire-blue eyes. The eye colour, real, the lashes not so much.

And you could hardly compare the green, scruffy mop on her head with my perfect blond curls.

Game, set and match to me. But she didn't seem at all fazed. She scrunched up her face in disgust.

"Are you lost?" she asked. "This isn't the Royal Opera, you know."

And that's when he kissed me.

Then he moved onto her.

She balanced against me as her hands ran up his chest, her back leaning against my side. Did she think I just existed for her convenience? That cheap perfume she wore would never come out of my top.

I moved away and she stumbled slightly but her lips stayed locked on his. So I grabbed his arm and pulled the two of them apart.

"Now listen here—"

"No, you listen. You've had your moment, now move along. I hate pushy groupies." He ran his fingers through his hair and glared at me.

"I'm not a groupie. I'm your manager!" I put my hands on my hips and glared right back.

I may have actually stamped my foot here, but he deserved it. He totally deserved to have my foot stamped at him. With that look of pure arrogant irritation he'd shot at me, he deserved more than foot stamping. He deserved a well-timed punch in the stomach – and I'd be just the woman to give it to him if I didn't think it'd ruin my manicure.

A guy carrying a drum squeezed past me, pressing me further against the wall. I sighed and waited for him to pass so I could finish what I had to say. The green-haired chick looked daggers at me for interrupting her, but seriously I'd done her a favour. She would thank me in years to come when she wised up.

Jack Colt ran his eyes over my designer outfit and high heels that looked so out of place in this dingy bar. His long eyelashes flickered as his eyes filled with a look of thinly veiled amusement.

"You're no manager, babe. Buy your shit and then get back to Rich Town and tell your friends all about your night slumming with the poor people."

It wasn't his words that got me angry but the way he grinned after he said it, as if I was someone he could dismiss.

I raised my hand and swung, ready to slap some sense into that annoying face of his, but he grabbed my wrist before I made contact.

"Don't even think about it, babe."

Then he dropped my hand as though it were something dirty.

He turned away, winking and grinning at someone at the bar.

"Megastar Management. Does that name ring any bells?"

He swung around.

"I'm Hannah Sorrento, the new manager."

"You're kidding, right? What's this, a new project for the bored little rich girl? Some kind of game? I'm busy, babe, so run back home."

I waited for him to drop his gaze. For all his bravado, I'd seen the flash in his eyes when I'd said my name. The Sorrento surname still held sway in this town. At least for now. If he wanted a showdown, I'd give him one. I didn't care that he'd kissed me. I didn't care that the look in his eyes made me feel as if I was beneath his contempt. I had one thing on my agenda. He tried that look again, shooting one hundred volts of pure arrogance my way, but I was prepared this time and shot it right back at him. We locked gazes and anyone coming between us would've been zapped like a bug.

I'd learnt negotiation on my father's knee and I'd learnt I had to be tougher than anyone. I knew whoever spoke first would lose.

You could only throw me for so long. My pulse was almost back to normal and my chest barely felt tight.

Finally, he walked away.

I stared after him. Nobody walked out on me. Nobody. I'd show him a thing or two. Mr Jack Colt belonged to me now and I had the papers to prove it.

A drum cymbal crashed as the next band went onstage in the front room and the chatter turned to screams. I shouted over the noise.

"Tuesday. Two o'clock at the coffee shop in the Sorrento Corporation building. I want to see the whole band turn up. We have things to discuss. Read your contract if you need to," I shouted over the top of the music.

He waved over his shoulder. I wasn't sure if it was agreement or dismissal.

Chapter 2

I waited at the dark shelter for the bus to turn up. I could hear the distant strains of music from the bar and the sounds of cars in the streets around me, but the beachside road that the bus took was deserted. A massive hedge separated me from the apartment building behind me and a large tree dimmed the glare of the streetlight. I could've sat in the bus shelter if some hoodlum hadn't smashed it up. The shattered glass crunched under my feet, probably doing untold damage to the soles of my shoes.

I hadn't considered the possibility of it being quite so creepy when I'd planned to catch the bus home. I figured I'd just turn up at the stop at the scheduled time and the bus would be there. It was already five minutes late, though. I wrapped my arms around myself and shivered. If only I'd brought a coat. I hadn't realised the wind would be so chilly or that I'd be standing around on the street.

The branches behind me rustled. I jumped. Maybe I screamed a little. Something lived in that bush. Something feral and rabid and hungry.

If only I had the money, I'd call a cab and get out of this place before that feral animal attacked me. How do people actually do anything if they have to wait around for buses all the time? No wonder they are poor, since they have to spend all their time waiting around and having to defend themselves from animal attacks. You might as well just be living in the wilderness and sleeping on the ground.

I checked the time again and walked to the curb to look for the bus but could not even see it in the distance so I paced back to the smashed-up shelter.

The wind seemed to be getting colder and still no bus. I pressed my fingers to my lips. They felt tender from *that man*. At least the thought of his arrogance made my blood boil enough to keep me warm. He'd better turn up to the meeting and he'd better lose the attitude. The world would be a much better place if people just did what I wanted.

My neck prickled, as if someone stood close to me. I tried to ignore it, telling myself to stop being so damn jumpy. Then I turned to find a huge man mountain hovering over me.

I yelped but no one heard me. He seriously reached up to the sky and took up the entire footpath. His filthy grey t-shirt stretched tight over his belly, with a solid ridge of white, hairy fat peeking out the bottom. A scraggy beard flowed down his face, full of food remains, and he looked me up and down as though he was a starving man who'd chanced upon a bacon sandwich. How he'd snuck up without me hearing him was a mystery.

His laugh made my blood run cold and he grunted something I couldn't understand through his broken teeth.

"Hey, Hagrid, look out of my way," I said, trying to get past him without actually touching him. My witty pop culture reference amused me and I smiled, thinking I'd tell my friends later.

Instead of looking out of the way, though, he pushed forward, making me stumble backwards and impale myself on the sharp branches. I backed away from him until I had nowhere left to retreat to. Why the hell hadn't that bus turned up?

"Get off me," I screamed again, but he moved closer, leaning over me. His breath stank of something that had died last week and his body – well. Fresh sweat gleamed on his skin but the odour was more of old sweat and backed-up sewage systems. I turned my face to get away from the full blast of him, the bile rising in my throat.

What could I do? Even if I screamed, who'd hear me? There was no one on the streets and the music pumping out of the bar would block any sound anyway. I definitely could not fight him.

"Take my bag," I said, thrusting it at him. "Take my bag and leave me alone."

He didn't even look at the precious handbag I was giving him. He reached for my shoulder, his hand like a big bear paw, and squeezed me tight. His eyes gleamed yellow in the glow from the flickering streetlight and he laughed like a lunatic.

I tried to twist my way out of his grasp and kicked his shin, hoping it'd give me a chance to run. Nothing registeredthough. He kept laughing and tightened his grip on me. His other hand fumbled with the fly on his jeans. I tried to squirm away from him but it was useless. I'd not cry. I never cry and I'd not give him the satisfaction.

He leaned in even closer. His tongue darted out, licking my cheek. His big meaty tongue touching my skin. All my insides shrivelled.

I swung my bag around, trying to knock him out with it, but he flung it out of my hand, scattering the contents all over the street, and grabbed me with both hands. I had no hope left. My head swam with dizziness and I hoped I'd pass out before he touched me any more. I whispered a prayer for someone to save me. A brave hero who'd send that freak running off in the darkness and take me in his arms and protect me.

"Oi, mister. Get away from her."

A voice. A girl's voice but still a voice. Maybe he'd attack her instead and I could run for safety.

A deluge of kicks and punches came out of nowhere. This chick didn't muck around. All I saw was a blur. Man Mountain's laugh turned into yelps as a boot kicked into him again and again. He dropped his hand from me and turned to defend himself.

I quickly ducked around the side of the shelter, not wanting him to grab me again and not wanting a stray punch to connect either. When he bent over in pain, I decided to risk running back to the bar. Then a boot-clad foot swung up between his legs and he shrieked like a little girl. When he spun around and limped off, I saw who my rescuer was.

"Sheesh, if I'd known it was you, I'd have let him get you," she said. It was the green-haired girl from the bar, only a beanie now covered the hair. She put her arm around my shoulder. "Only kidding, couldn't let a monster like that get away with shit."

"Thanks," I said, a nervous giggle rising up in me. I moved away and dusted myself down. I wasn't fond of being embraced by strangers, even if they had just rescued me.

She looked me up and down, then reached over and picked a twig out of my hair.

"You don't exactly look like the type that catches the bus," she said. "Here, I'll help you pick up your stuff."

I shrugged. I wasn't exactly going to go into the circumstances that led to me being a passenger on the 552 bus on a Saturday night to a complete stranger.

"Do you wanna call the cops?" she asked, retrieving a lipstick that had rolled into the gutter.

I shook my head, remembering Frank's advice to stay out of trouble.

"Prolly a good thing. It'd mean hours of filling out paperwork and they wouldn't do anything anyway. He was a nasty bugger, wasn't he?"

She fumbled in her bag.

"Want a cig?" she asked. "It'll calm you down."

I shook my head and leaned against the pole of the bus stop to steady myself.

"Well, I hope you aren't one of those sanctimonious bitches who gets all uptight if I smoke. Because I'm going to light up, and you should be damn grateful cos everyone knows the bus never turns up until you light up a cigarette anyway." She sparked her lighter and dragged on her cigarette.

"It's fine. The bus is late anyway." I looked at my watch, then gazed over at the timetable.

"Hells, love. You really are naive if you believe the bus timetable. There's no 'time' in timetable or some shit like that. The bus turns up when it turns up. It's like Zen or Buddhism or whatever that religion is that believes in shit like that. One time, I waited over a half hour, then the bloody bus just went whizzing past me and I had to wait for the next one. Bloody shits. Hey, is it true? Are you really the manager of Storm? I love those guys."

I wondered when she actually found time to breathe but her chatter helped me feel safer, even though I kept scanning the street for freaks.

"Yeah, it seems that way."

"No offence, love, but you don't really look like a manager. You don't look like you'd know the first thing about rock. In that get-up you look like you should be going to the opera or the races or something. Next time, let me pick your outfit."

I hoped my smile looked sincere. Actually, she didn't look too bad once you got over the bright green hair. She'd be pretty with the right grooming.

"See, told you the bus would turn up when I lit up a smoke." She took a last desperate drag of her cigarette.

I turned to see the bus pulling up. I got on and swiped my card, then took a seat and prepared to put in my headphones, but she sat beside me and kept talking.

This was only the second time in my life I'd caught the bus and already I'd realised that no matter what, crazies will sit next to you and talk your ears off. I figured it was better to let her sit beside me. At least she didn't smell or drool – and she had rescued me from that oaf.

"Name's Angie, by the way. And you are Hannah. I heard you say that at the bar."

I nodded.

"Where you going?"

I told her.

"You live near me. Cool. If you are going to manage the guys, I have a few suggestions if you don't mind me telling you. To be honest, you don't look like you know much about managing a band and I reckon I'd be really tops at that kind of thing."

I listened to her because she sounded like she knew what she was talking about. And she was right, I knew nothing about managing a band, but my motives were more like unmanaging them.

Chapter 3

The stupid garbage truck pulled me out of a very hot dream the next morning. It was all sexy and sweaty and – I refused to dream about Jack Colt. I refused to imagine his hands running down my body, sending divine shivers through me. I refused to think about his long fingers caressing my skin. I wouldn't even think about his mouth or tongue or the things they did to me in my dream. I would not think about Jack Colt in that way at all. Instead I'd think about nice things, like my boyfriend, Tom.

But the dream stuck to the edges of my brain and I kept getting flashes of stupid Jack Colt doing that thing he did with his hips. And the leather stretched tight around his thighs. The way he strutted around like he owned the place. Mr Jack Colt – if that indeed was his real name, because it sounded pretty fake to me – thought he was a sex god, but not in my book. I tried to bring up images of Tom instead but couldn't picture him clearly. I could remember the clothes he wore and the aftershave he used but I could not remember the emotions he made me feel. It hadn't been that long but already his face had faded in my mind like an old photo.

I sat up in bed, then thought about going back to sleep. When I slept, I could pretend I had my old life back. I'd get up and put together a fabulous outfit, then go to meet my friends for coffee. Often, someone would want to take my photo for the campus fashion blog. And that was all before the first lecture.

But the hard, rickety single bed that doubled as a couch gave me a backache and, every time I turned in my sleep, the bed creaked and woke me up. I'd not had a decent sleep since I'd moved in. I wasn't totally convinced this place didn't have some kind of bugs either, even though I'd gone through three bottles of bug spray when I first got here.

You could almost reach the kitchen from the bed. Well, if you could call it a kitchen, I suppose. A tiny bar fridge that hummed and rattled all night and smelt like maybe three years ago someone had spilt milk in it and never cleaned it out. There was a hotplate and a kind of sink with cold water. If I wanted hot water, I had to boil it on the hotplate. Someone had left some plates and saucepans on a shelf under the sink. As much as I hated the idea of using someone else's manky stuff, I couldn't afford to replace them.

I didn't cook anything here anyway. The whole place would reek if I tried cooking and the smell would get into my clothes, which filled most of the room. My regular clothes hung on a rack at the end of my bed that had already collapsed about three times since I'd been there, usually during the night, waking me up in fright. I'd packed the really good stuff away in boxes under my bed so it stayed decent. I had boxes of shoes and handbags stacked up around the room. It looked like a disorganised wardrobe, although the entire room would have fit inside my wardrobe back home. I'd tried not to think too much about how orderly things used to be. How everything was colour-coded and matched and hung correctly. When I left for uni, I'd thought I had it tough with just a single walk-in robe, but this place, this place was a slum. Literally. A literal slum. These clothes were all I had to comfort me and I couldn't care for them in the way they needed to be cared for. It broke my heart.

I needed those clothes. I needed them to look good and to smell good. Imagine if I gave off an odour of fried onions or garlic? I'd never fool anyone into thinking I was still a princess. But already I had a basket of things that needed dry cleaning, and dry cleaning cost money.

Someone shuffled down the hallway to the bathroom. I'd stay in my room until they were done.

A draught blew through the gaps in the floorboards, chilling my feet when I got out of bed. The walls had traces of bright pink shining through the chipped white paint and a speckled pattern of mildew. The woman in the room next door muttered to herself and I could hear her at night when I tried to sleep. And sometimes I could hear the girl down the hallway and her thug boyfriend making weird noises. I'd cover my head with my pillow and try not to think about what they were doing.

But one day, this would be over. One day, I'd be back in the house, where thick carpets muffled all sounds and the sun reflected off the pool and everything I wanted would be mine with just a snap of my fingers. This would be a nightmare.

I should call Tom. If he didn't hear from me, he'd get worried, and the last thing I wanted was for him to come down here looking for me. All he knew was that I'd dropped out of school to find myself and had moved back home for a while. I'd give him a ring later when he'd finished classes to keep him happy. Lately, he'd been busy when I tried to call him. I didn't have much to say to him anyway.

Until then, I had to get out of this place. If I sat in this room all day, staring at those four walls, I'd go crazy. I needed to at least go out and get coffee and forget for a moment that I didn't really have any place to go.

When I heard the footsteps shuffle back to a room and the door close, I grabbed my stuff and headed to the communal bathroom, carefully locking my room behind me. The bathroom was none too clean and I thought one of the losers in this place could at least give it a scrub.

The hot water in the shower washed away all the grime, the places that Jack Colt's hands had touched me, thinking that his slight attention would be a way to make more sales, it seemed. The spot on the back of my neck where he'd caressed me, I didn't care about that at all. I let the soap and water carry away any traces. And I scrubbed the place on my thigh where his leg had pressed against mine. I didn't need any reminder of that.

I planned on turning up to the meeting on Tuesday all businesslike and professional and like I'd forgotten he'd even kissed me. That would teach him a valuable lesson. I'd put my case to them and hopefully they'd see sense. Then I'd walk away with a bundle of money and could go back and finish my degree and wait for Dad to return. I'd even forgive him for dumping me in this mess.

I dried myself off, then popped my head out the door to make sure no one was around. I really didn't fancy running into anyone in the hallway and standing around having a chat about their back pains or what boringly awful things they'd been doing all day.

The floor creaked as I ran along the hallway and I thought I heard a door open but I darted into my room so quickly no one saw me. I began getting ready to go out.

I picked up a bottle of moisturiser and shook it. Nothing came out. I squeezed and a dollop splattered onto my hand. I shook it some more. It was almost empty. No way. I needed that moisturiser. It made my skin soft and glowing and it was one of the few brands my sensitive skin could handle. How much was a bottle of moisturiser anyway? About three hundred dollars.

Then I realised I could not afford to buy more. How does a person get to this state? Not being able to afford life's essentials. Surely poor people needed moisturiser too, or they'd all have dry, flaky skin. I had to find out about this.

Once I was clean and dressed, I got out the folder Frank had given me. It was fat and packed full of notes – all the records and financial statements of Megastar Management. I packed it into my bag and headed out to the café on the corner to make sense of it all. I had five hundred dollars in the bank, which meant I could afford to pay rent for the next few weeks and eat and maybe buy one coffee a day. I'd make that coffee last for a long time and not even look at the bagels or the fries.

I'd never really thought before about the concept of *afford* or *can't afford*, just *want* or *don't want*. Now, I had to scribble away on pieces of paper, working out budgets and how to survive. I could do this. Like Dad said, I had to be stronger than anyone, and living for two weeks on a budget couldn't be too bad. Surely it wouldn't be any longer. The end of those two weeks loomed in front of me like a closed door. If Dad didn't come back and open it... well, I wouldn't think about that.

When I got to the café, I sat in a corner booth with red vinyl seats. Planters of ferns hung from the ceiling and I wasn't sure if they were going for a retro '70s look or if they just hadn't redecorated since the '70s. The counter with its tempting display case of cakes ran along one side of the room, while the booths along the side and tables at the front looked out onto the street. There were more tables outside, but they were always full of people who might be hipsters or might be homeless. I couldn't tell the difference.

I'd never even been to this part of town before I'd had to move here. I didn't realise it existed. But the rent was cheap and they hadn't asked any questions when I moved in. They just took the money and gave me a key.

I opened the file and checked the papers. I'd gone through them before but hoped I'd find something, anything that meant I could make money. It seemed Megastar Management had once been a money-making concern but then Dad had turned his attention to other things and the business just floated along. The only acts still on the roster were Storm and some oldies that never played any more.

The only real asset of the company, if you could even call it an asset, was the Storm contract. It had to be worth something. I'd started on Plan A; now I needed to work on Plan B, just in case.

As I sipped my coffee, I wondered if I could do this. I didn't know anything about managing a band. How much could they earn from playing a bar like they did last night? How many people were there? Who had even been organising this stuff for the past year?

"Hiya, what are you doing?"

Angie slid into the booth. She was all grins and wearing another Storm t-shirt, her hair in pigtail bunches all over her head and bright blue lining her eyes.

She'd talked my ear off on the bus ride home, mostly fangirl gushing, then we'd got off at the same stop and realised we lived really close to each other. Still, when she'd said, "See you around," I hadn't expected it to be quite so soon. She would be much better at managing the band than me and I wondered if she had any money.

"Okay, since you need some help, I've set up a website." She pulled out her phone and showed me what she'd done. It looked fantastic. I grinned, then remembered.

"Didn't they have a website before?" God, who doesn't have a website in the twenty-first century? No wonder these guys made no money.

"Yeah, they had one but it was shit. It looked like it'd been made in Geocities and was never updated."

"You know we have no money to pay you."

"That's okay," she said. "I'm happy to do it. For love. Love of a groupie for her band is the purest love of all, right? You don't expect money or even for your love to be returned. All you want is for them to keep on doing what they do. Okay, and maybe one day notice you in the crowd and realise you are their one true love and live happily ever after..."

I laughed. "Do you think anyone is going to live happily ever after with Jack Colt?"

She waved to the waitress for a coffee and sighed.

"Word on the street is no. Word on the street is that he has a two-week limit. That's the longest any woman has caught him for. But hey, maybe two weeks is better than nothing. It would be the best two weeks of my life."

The waitress set down the coffee.

"You having another?" she asked me.

I looked at my empty cup. I wanted more coffee. I really needed more coffee. Screw it. Coffee is an investment, right? You can't work without coffee, so if I deprived myself, I'd end up not making a profit. I understand business. You only get out if you put in.

"So," I asked her, "have you ever dated him?"

She leaned on the table with a wistful look in her eyes. "Not yet, but you know what they say – it doesn't matter if there's a queue, so long as it's moving."

I laughed. She didn't mind laying it all out there. It was something I could never do. Even when people asked me about Tom, I never liked to talk about my private business.

She folded her hands and I noticed the chunky silver rings on her fingers. I looked at my hand with just the thin band that had been my grandmother's on it. It'd been her wedding ring.

"He thinks he's a badass. Is he really that amazing?"

"Hey, he kissed you too. Didn't you feel it? The thunder. The bolts of lightning. They are called Storm for a reason! That welling up like fireworks about to explode? The sounds of cannons firing... POW! If he can do that with just a kiss, imagine what his cock is like."

I spurted out my coffee. Imagining Jack Colt's cock was not my intention, although it'd be long and thin, like his fingers and...

"What about the rest of the band?"

"Well, there's Eric, the bass player. He's half-Korean and pretty quiet most of the time. He doesn't really let on what he's thinking but he takes the music seriously. I think he does most of the stuff for the band because their management is pretty slack. Oops, sorry."

"That's okay. Go on."

"He's a graphic designer and so he does most of the graphics for the band, like this." She held out the picture on the front of the t-shirt to demonstrate. "Hey, can you get the files from him? I can add them to the site. And then there's Spud. He's okay. Not real bright but he's a great drummer. I think he could be gay. Well, maybe. I've never seen him with a chick before."

I wondered if he was the one carrying the drum into the backroom.

"Ha, check this out. We've got a hundred followers on the site already. Bonus. Do we need a Twitter? We need Twitter, right? And Facebook. A band is nothing without social media these days. Hey, it's okay me doing this? I mean, I don't wanna step on your toes or anything."

"No, it's okay, really." Like I wouldn't want her doing all this work for free.

"There's another thing. I really feel like I'm being pushy now and..."

I looked at her encouragingly. I'd not known Angie for long but already it got me worried when she was nervous about broaching a subject. This girl had the motormouth to end all motormouths.

"Can I make a video clip? Please say I can? I need a project for my final assessment and if I had to pick any project at all this would be my uttermost dream project. In fact, I do dream about it all the time. I can direct it and I've a few friends who can film and do lighting and all that and I will do the most top-notch professional job of editing it all together. Please say yes. Please say I can do it. Please, please."

She tried to look at me with puppy dog eyes, her chin rested on hands covered in some hot-pink-and-black glove things. I'm not sure how puppy-like they were, though. I calculated how that would affect my plans. Good thing? Bad thing?

"We could get them to dress up. Or maybe not. Jack would hate it. He'd probably want to sack you as manager."

"We'll do it."

She squealed.

"I also have some notes about where the band should play. I'm an idiot. Of course, you'd know all this stuff already but I really, really think they should be playing bigger venues. You saw how crowded the bar was last night and they weren't even headlining. In fact, half the crowd left before the main band. So I've made a few suggestions here. Maybe you've tried to book them already. I didn't call the venues or anything, honest."

I folded the notes and put them in my bag. They might come in handy.

"By the way, I need to ask you something. Where do..." I couldn't actually say poor people, could I? I mean, people get a bit upset about that kind of thing. What was the polite way of saying it? "Where do you buy moisturiser when you don't have much money? Is there something that's good but not too expensive?"

She gave me a strange look.

"You don't exactly look poor, you know."

"Yeah, well, all my money is tied up at the moment. I don't have a lot of cash to spend."

"Ah, shit. See, it's going to take about a thousand dollars to make the video. We can do it cheap but we need to hire lights and a space. If we want it to look good, I reckon a grand is the absolute minimum."

"That might be difficult." I hated to say it. I'd never once in my life had to tell anyone I'd not been able to do something because I couldn't afford it.

We both sighed.

She rummaged around in her handbag – seriously that bag was the hugest thing I'd ever seen – and handed me a fistful of sachets.

"Here, take these. I get them free."

I took them. That was enough moisturiser to last me a few weeks. Surely everything would be back to normal by then anyway. I'd never heard of the brand, though. I hoped it wouldn't make me break out in hives.

"Thanks. Where do you get this stuff?"

"Well, it's my job. Hey, wait, do you want to earn some easy money?"

I raised my eyebrow. I might be down on my luck but I wasn't *that* down on my luck. Easy money usually meant one thing and I wasn't desperate enough for that.

"Don't worry, it's nothing dodgy. Easy as. I'm a promo girl. You know, those chicks you see at the train stations handing out free samples. It pays all right money and they are always looking for people. So long as you are okay-looking and not a complete social retard. It's just a couple of hours in the morning, then again at night when everyone is knocking off work. You'll be a shoo-in."

I actually didn't know anything about people handing out free samples at the station. I'd never even been to the train station.

"I can't do that!"

"Why not? You said your money is tied up. Hey, is someone holding it for ransom?" She exploded into giggles at that, slapping the table. I tried to grin but she wasn't far wrong.

"And you get to keep heaps of samples, sometimes even chocolate or that moisturiser. Of course, sometimes it's shit stuff like discount coupons or crappy health food bars. Still, I'll just call Sammy and let him know to expect you."

"Wow, you're like my fairy godmother or something."

"Yeah, 'or something' is more like it. And anyway, the guys should reimburse you for the video production costs, right? I mean, it's for them. A couple of good gigs would just about cover the cost."

I looked at the menu while she talked on the phone. Surely, if I was going to work, I could justify buying something to eat.

She covered the phone. "You don't mind dressing up as a tree frog, do you?"

Chapter 4

I turned up to the meeting wearing a red shift dress. I figured red is the colour of power and I needed power. They would never know about the pile of about fifty outfits I'd tried on before I left home. Not that I was nervous or anything. I wasn't even sure if they'd turn up. I'd probably be stuck waiting for them for an hour and then give up and go home.

To add to the stress, I'd stupidly arranged to meet them at Sorrento, Inc. headquarters. The office building that *had* been the site of Dad's now ex-company. Hopefully they wouldn't notice the empty spots on the signboard or the lack of people around. I really, really didn't want to run into people I knew. As much as it'd been kept out of the news, people there would know all about the scandal. They probably knew more than I did. Of course, most of the business had been wound down now, but that didn't mean I'd not run into anyone.

As a safety measure, I donned my massive sunglasses.

The only reason I'd picked this café was that I knew they'd know it. I'd had to think of something off the top of my head when I gave Jack Colt a meeting place and this was the only place I could think of at the time.

My eyes swept around the café, checking if the band were there but not expecting to see them. I almost jumped to see them sitting in the corner, with guitar cases blocking the walkway between the tables.

At this time of day, there were only a few other people there. They sat in their suits on the other side of the café as though wanting to put as much distance between themselves and the band as possible.

Jack Colt lounged back in his low chair, his leg over the arm. He looked up as I walked toward them but didn't acknowledge me. He just kept talking to the other two as though I were a random person walking in off the street.

Eric sat in the seat by the window and Spud leaned back with his feet on the coffee table in the middle.

I walked over and stood by them.

The bass player, Eric, gave me a smile.

"You must be Eric," I said and smiled back. "And you are Spud."

"Greg," he grunted but didn't look up. Then he and Jack continued talking about amplifiers and distortion pedals, whatever they were. What was the point of them even turning up to this meeting if they were going to ignore me anyway? They might as well have not come.

I ordered a glass of wine and cleared my throat, then launched into my spiel.

"Okay, I guess you want to know what this meeting is all about?"

Eric brushed his long fringe out of his eyes, then fumbled in the bag at his feet and pulled out a clip to pin it back. That would look effeminate on most guys but not on him.

"The guy from Mega came to a few gigs, then got us all excited about a contract. So we signed, then nothing. We barely heard from him again. I called him a few times and he said he was talking to A&R people and had a few big things lined up but never came through with anything."

"Well, I'm not..."

Jack adjusted himself in his seat. I turned to see his crotch pointed directly towards my face. With the outline of his cock pressing against those tight leather pants. He knew exactly what he was doing; he was doing it to fluster me. The look in his eyes held a direct challenge. I took a deep breath and refused to play his stupid game, even though my heartbeat did all kinds of crazy things. I looked him square in the eye, determined my gaze would not move any lower.

"I'm not your old manager," I said. "Now you have two options. Either do as I say or buy out the management contract yourselves."

I stared back at Jack Colt, determined to let him know I wasn't shaken by him. His mouth twitched at the edges then he rumbled into laughter.

"Oh, that's clever, babes, trying to make us pay for something we already have. You appear out of nowhere and think you can be our manager, then want *us* to pay *you* not to do it?"

The laughter didn't extend to his eyes, still dark and cold and locked onto mine.

I pulled a copy of the contract out of my bag.

"You signed here." I stabbed at the paper with my finger. "This is a legal document. I am the legal owner of Megastar Management. I have legal authority to represent you. I can make bookings in your name. I can sign contracts in your name."

Jack Colt shrugged.

"What can I say, babes? We were young, starry-eyed musos back then. We thought that guy was going to make us the next big thing."

He gave Spud a look and they both laughed. Seriously, if he didn't stop calling me babe, I'd punch him in the stomach.

I leaned towards him.

"Excuse me. One of us here is studying law at a prestigious university and the other... well..." I gave him a look letting him know I meant business. "You don't want to mess with me."

"So, if we did buy out the contract, how much would that be?"

I smiled at Eric. At least he had some common decency and manners. Then I named a figure and all three of them laughed.

"You really think we are worth that?"

"We're worth it, but we aren't paying."

"We don't have any money anyway, do we, Jack?" added Spud.

I'd been expecting this but I'd hoped they would play along. It'd have been the perfect solution to everything if they'd just agreed. Of course, Angie had said they had no money. Eric was the only one with a job but she'd told me something else too. A few years ago, Jack had been up on assault charges. Shit had gone down at a gig, was how Angie put it. It had looked like Jack would go to jail. Then, suddenly, he'd been released and nothing more was said about it. It took serious money to do that kind of thing. There had to be a money trail somehow.

Frank had said they wouldn't pay up that easily. It looked like I'd have to move on to Plan B – make the idea of getting rid of me a helluva lot more attractive.

"Make them think you're a dingbat," Frank had told me. "No one wants a dingbat as a manager."

I looked at the three of them, still laughing, and I sipped my wine.

"Okay, I gave you the option. Remember that, because it will cost you a ton of money if you want to get out of this contract later on."

I got the three files out of my bag and handed them around. Eric and Spud took theirs but Jack continued to stare at me until the back of my neck prickled. I set the folder on the coffee table in front of him.

"Why do we need a manager, anyway? We turn up, we play our music and that's it. Managers are for pretty boy bands who need someone to tell them what to do."

I twisted the ring on my finger and looked out the window. I figured he'd try to undermine me.

"Pretty boy bands make a lot of money. If you look at One Direction, for example—"

"What? That proves it." He rolled his eyes. "You know nothing about what we do. Nothing."

I would not lose my temper. I would not say anything stupid. I would stay cool and businesslike. Even with the blood pumping hard in my temples.

"What about all the administration? You need someone to do that so you can concentrate on the music."

Jack Colt leaned forward, his face so close to mine, I could feel his breath on my skin. I wanted to back away before my stomach flip-flopped out of my body but I refused to move.

"Understand this, babe." He said the "babe" as though hurling an insult. "There is no administration. There is no anything. Eric makes a few calls and we play. No one needs to take a cut of that."

"There's no administration because you aren't going anywhere." I took a swig of my wine. "Don't you have any ambition? Don't you want to play festivals?" I took the sheet of paper Angie had given me from my bag and straightened it against my knee. "What about the Metropolis? Don't you want to play somewhere like that?"

He rolled his eyes again.

"We've tried to get gigs at the Metropolis before," said Eric, "and, well..."

"Well, listen, babe, if you can book us a gig at the Metropolis by the end of the week, we'll go along with this shit. Otherwise, you can tear that stupid contract into bits."

He smirked at Spud as if to say there was no way I could do it. Like I had no ability to pick up the phone and call someone and set up a gig. I was totally capable of doing all that and more.

I rubbed my grandmother's ring again, needing the comforting reassurance of it, and sat forward in my chair. The cold challenge in his eyes said I couldn't do it.

"I don't need to prove anything." I picked up the contract again.

"You might have your contract and all your legal bunk but you can't force us to do anything. What are you going to do if we don't show up? Throw us over your shoulder and force us to play? Not going to happen. Take us to court and sue us? You can't get blood out of a stone, babe, and we have no money to pay."

I gulped. That was my bluff. I had no legal standing and I hoped they wouldn't realise. He was one hundred per cent right. They could walk away right now and I'd have nothing, not even the management company to sell.

"I'll take your challenge. By the end of the week, you say. Fine. And then you'll follow the plan." I picked up the folder sitting on the table and waved it at him. "You'll play the places I say and turn this band into a paying proposition."

"If you can swing it." He snorted, not believing I could do it.

"Have you ever managed a band before, rich girl? They don't let just anyone play the Metro, you know." Spud snorted.

Eric pulled a bunch of CDs out of his bag and handed them to me.

"You might need these. They are our demos. And I'll send you some bios too."

"Oh yeah, that reminds me. We have a website now. And maybe one of you could do some Twittering and stuff like that. You need a social media presence, you know."

Jack Colt coughed and I turned, completely forgetting about *that* thing. My eyes had gone straight to his groin with its unmistakable bulge. I blushed and tried to will myself to stop but the more I tried not to blush the more my face burned.

"I don't Twitter."

"And we are making a music video." I figured that would put the ball back in my court.

"So, which of our songs do you intend to make this clip for? I assume that as our manager, you are fully aware of our entire repertoire."

"As your manager, I don't need to know your songs. I deal with the business side, not the music. And, if you don't like it, remember I gave you the option of buying me out."

But he ignored me and stood up. Picking up his guitar case, he nodded at the others.

"We have shit to do."

He walked off but Eric waited.

"We're doing a gig tonight. It's just going to be small but it'd be worth you coming along. You really might want to listen to some of our stuff."

I stared at Jack Colt's back as he leaned on the counter paying the bill. "I don't know if I'd be welcome."

"Oh, don't worry about Jack. He has some issues but it's not like he's in charge of who comes to see the band play. I'd really like you to come along."

He looked up at me through the fringe of hair that had come loose from the clip with such a cute look in his eyes, I could hardly say no. In fact, everything about Eric was cute. From his hair to the black nail polish on the tips of his fingernails that peeked out of the stretched sleeves of his sweater. He grinned.

"You'll come? Oh, that's so unreal. Hurry up or they'll go without us."

I followed after Eric but I wasn't sure if I was doing the right thing.

Chapter 5

We rushed through the streets, trying to keep up with Jack and Spud. I'd have thought they'd have a van for all their gear but they just had the guitar cases. He weaved through cobblestoned backstreets until I had no idea where I was. Eric talked to me while we walked but my attention kept slipping to Jack Colt's leather-wrapped buttocks. Those pants left nothing to the imagination and he sure had a sexy curve. I didn't want to look but he walked in front of me, practically forcing me to.

"Watch out," Eric said.

"Huh?"

"Don't fall for Jack. He's not a steady relationship kind of guy. I'd hate to see you get hurt."

"You're kidding, right? He's a jerk."

"He's not a jerk, he's just got some serious baggage. But I shouldn't really talk about that."

"What makes you think I'd fall for him? You saw us back there. I'm more likely to kill him than fall for him."

"You're the kind of girl who's had her own way for most of her life. Then you meet a guy like Jack who stands up to you. You can mistake that kind of thing for love."

"Not me, buddy."

Eric shot me a shy grin and I couldn't help but grin back.

When we got to the bar, Eric told the owner I was their manager.

"Not yet, she isn't."

"She's our manager at the moment and she's on the guest list."

The owner let me in without paying and got me a glass of wine for free while the band set up. This bar looked so different from the one the other night. The stage was low-key, with red velvet curtains lining it. The room had tables and chairs, not just standing room, and a mural of a night sky covered the ceiling. Also, the place didn't reek of stale beer and sweat.

I sat at the bar drinking my wine as people filled the place up. It was a decent-sized crowd for a Tuesday night. I tried to look entertained while I sat there but really it was not that interesting. I got out my phone and played a game of solitaire, wishing they'd hurry up and get started. I'd have ordered another drink if I'd thought I could afford it.

Eric popped up beside me, ordering a round of beers, and told the barman to put another wine on the tab for me too.

"Thanks."

"No worries. We'll be onstage in five minutes or so. If you want any more, just let Charlie know. He'll be happy to put it on the tab for you."

I nodded but to be honest, I didn't really drink that much. Charlie grinned at me.

"Here, try this. I've been experimenting with cocktails. I reckon you'll like it."

Since I didn't have much to do but sit there and drink, I figured I might as well give it a try. I took a sip. It was sweet and fruity.

I looked around for Angie but couldn't see her in the crowd. I thought she might be here for something like this but the crowd seemed a bit older than the other night.

Everyone clapped as the guys went onstage. They didn't cheer or get raucous, though.

When Jack Colt began singing, I turned to the stage. He sat on the stool quietly. No posturing or over-the-top moves, just him sitting there singing, with Eric playing along and Spud in the background. A soft spotlight shone on him as he sang about love and hurts and the things he couldn't get over.

His hair flopped onto his face as he leaned over his guitar but every so often he'd look up at the crowd, his eyes expressing the pain of the song he sang.

Charlie handed me another cocktail and I felt warm inside. Maybe Jack Colt wasn't so bad after all. When I saw him like this, he seemed vulnerable. Maybe he just needed someone to take care of him, to lie beside him and stroke his hair until that hurt in his eyes went away.

What was I thinking? I shook my head to clear that thought. It was his onstage image, acting like that to win across the audience. I knew better. I just had to remind myself what a jerk he'd been.

After a few songs, Eric left the stage and came to sit by me. Jack continued on alone.

"It's magic, isn't it?" he said. He looked at Jack.

"He's not bad." To be honest, the other night the band had struck me as a cacophony of noise. This was different, though. They really had something.

"What are you drinking?"

I took another sip. "It's some new cocktail. Want to try it?"

"No, thanks. I'll stick to beer."

"Why are you being nice to me? The other two hate me."

"They don't hate you. Maybe it's a bit of a shock for them, having some chick show up claiming to be our manager. We've had a lot of disappointments. A few times we've nearly been signed to a label, then it fell through. And Jack, well, he has this thing. This kind of 'it's my way or the highway' thing, you know. He doesn't like to compromise and that means we might not be as good a deal to take on as some of these younger kids who do as they're told."

I nodded. I could see what he meant. Jack Colt was going to be tough to deal with.

"Well, I've got to get back onstage. Take it easy with those fruity drinks. It'd be kinda embarrassing for our manager to get drunk and make a scene."

As he walked off, I wondered how embarrassing. Embarrassing enough for them to want to get rid of me? Maybe I could get a little tipsy.

I got up to go to the bathroom. I'd gotten really hot sitting at the bar and needed to cool down. As I touched up my make-up, a girl came out of the cubicle and stood at the sink beside me.

"Great set tonight, huh."

I nodded. She had on a fabulous skirt. It looked just like one I used to have the year before. Almost identical, in fact.

"Love your skirt," I said.

"Thanks," she shouted of the sound of the hand dryer. "I got it from that designer recycle place near the Arts Centre."

"Designer recycle? What the hell is that?"

"You know, where rich people go to sell their old clothes."

I nodded, but the idea didn't compute. Rich people don't sell their old clothes. They throw them out or give them away or something. I didn't even know. I just gave them to the maid to deal with.

Hey, those bloody maids – they'd been selling off my clothes and now this chick wore my skirt. And it was an awesome skirt. I wanted it back. I guess I couldn't tell her that, though.

I returned to the bar in a shitty mood. You couldn't trust anyone nowadays. I ordered another drink. It shouldn't matter. I hadn't wanted the skirt anyway, but that didn't mean I wanted someone else wearing it. Especially someone who looked awesome in it. Not more awesome than me, but still awesome. I should've put the idea out of my head. After all, there wasn't much I could do about it. I couldn't even sack the maids since they were already out of jobs. I sipped my cocktail and brooded, with Jack Colt singing a blues song to match my mood. At times, his voice had the effect of a cheese grater being run over my heart.

So rough, so raw, holding out all those horrible things that people really should hide away deep inside.

It was his eyes that got people, I decided. Even from the distance of the bar, you could tell that. It felt like he could see into your soul and hunt out the hurts in there and give you comfort. I couldn't reconcile that with the man parading his cock earlier. He was the one putting the hurts in my heart to start with. If I didn't know better, I'd have thought this guy was someone I wanted to get close to. Stupid music. Still, it was magic and, for a moment, I thought it might actually be worth working with this band.

When the band finished playing, I cheered and screamed until I noticed a few people staring at me. Maybe I'd been a bit loud, but then I'd planned to get tipsy.

Since I had no idea how to get home, I waited for the guys to pack up their gear. They could at least tell me how to get to the station. A couple of guys stood by me at the bar and offered to buy me drinks. I wouldn't say no. I felt better than I had in days. Those drinks were good. The hard edges of my world melted away in a fuzzy blur. What did I care about money and rock stars and people selling my clothes? Nothing and no one could hurt me.

How much do you need to drink to get a bit tipsy, anyway? I'd not had lunch but I'd only had what, two or three drinks? And the glass of wine when I came in.

When Jack and Eric came to the bar, I swung around on my stool.

"Hey, Jack. Hey, Eric."

"You've had too much to drink," Jack said. "You should get home."

He moved in and leaned on the bar, waving at the barman to get him a beer.

"I don't know how to get home."

"You could get a taxi."

"Don't have any money to get a taxi."

He groaned.

"Don't groan at me." I wagged my finger at him. "I'm fine. You just have to tell me how to get back to the city and I'll find my way from there."

I stood up and very carefully gathered up my bag. I'd walk straight out the door. I could do that without looking drunk and I could talk very clearly without slurring my words.

"I'm fine. Fine. Don't worry about me," I said, then banged into the man standing behind me.

I brushed him down.

"Sorry, sorry. Oops, why are you standing there?" I giggled. It seemed crazy funny that I'd swung around straight into this strange man.

Jack pulled my arm. "You need to sober up."

"I'm fine," I said.

He snorted like he didn't believe me. But I was fine. I just felt a bit sleepy and everything looked blurry and he looked really fine in those tight leather pants. I really should tell him that. Before I could speak, though, he'd grabbed me.

"You aren't going to kiss me again. I'm not your groupie. You don't need to kiss me."

I waited with my face turned towards him but he pulled my arm and dragged me across the room. I struggled but couldn't get free of his grip.

"Stop struggling," he hissed. "You are just making a fool of yourself."

He opened the door to the small room behind the stage and dumped me down in a chair.

"Just wait there until we are ready to leave, then we'll sort something out about getting you home."

"Yes, sir," I said giving him a salute.

He left the room and I looked around. Oh, someone had left some beer behind. I decided to drink it. After all, who was he to tell me not to drink? I could drink if I wanted to. He wasn't the boss of me.

Making a fool of myself? Hadn't that been my plan. To make them think I was a dingbat? I should go out there and show them just how dingbat I could be. Except I felt a little sleepy. They'd left their jackets and stuff on the bench in the corner. I could just curl up there and have a little nap until they were ready to tell me how to get home.

The next thing I knew there were voices. Voices in my dream? No, outside me.

"What are we going to do with her?"

"She hasn't thrown up on my coat, has she? Because if she has, I'll kill her."

"No, she's okay. She's just resting. We'll have to take her with us. Unless you want to go through her bag and find her address."

I wanted to sit up and tell them I was fine and I knew my own address but it seemed like such an effort to move and I could tell them after I finished sleeping.

"Come on, Hannah. The bar's closing."

"Great manager, huh. She flakes after a few drinks." That was Spud's voice.

"Like you can talk, Spud. Remember that time you threw up after the gig down the coast? Miserablest bastard alive in the van on the way back. 'Stop the car, stop the car...' And those cocktails looked a bit lethal."

I silently thanked Eric and tried to get myself to sit up. If they let me sleep for little bit longer, I'd be okay.

"We'll get some coffee into her when we get home and she'll sober up."

"Coffee!" I sat up. "Did someone say coffee?"

The next thing I knew, strong arms wrapped around me and lifted me.

"Can you walk?"

I nodded but I wasn't really sure. I leaned in against his warm, strong chest. In his arms, I felt safe and happy. But they were mean and kept making me move around and then we were outside and it was cold and I felt a coat being wrapped around my shoulders. I slumped against something that I thought was a wall but it moved. And then we were in a car and we were going somewhere and the lights of the city looked pretty and blurry as I pressed my face against the cold glass. When we crossed the river, I wanted to tell them we were going the wrong way. I didn't live across the river. Not any more. I lived in... where did I live?

Chapter 6

By the time the taxi pulled up, my head had cleared and I could walk on my own.

"Whose place is this?" I asked.

"Mine," said Eric. "Mine and Jack's."

If I'd thought about where they lived, I'd have expected something much grungier than this. We walked into a huge, open living area with a pair of massive sofas and a large-screen TV. To one side was an open kitchen area, and to the other side, French doors opening out to a small courtyard. This definitely was not the type of place you could afford on a struggling rock star's income. This was some prime industrial chic real estate. And they'd said they didn't have the money to buy out the contract.

"Want a drink?" Eric asked.

"There was talk of coffee," I replied.

Then the doorbell rang and people piled into the apartment. Eric disappeared for a while and came back with more promises of coffee.

I sat on the sofa, still feeling a bit out of it. While I'd sobered up a bit, my head felt groggy and heavy.

There were about twenty people in the room, with more coming in behind them. Lots of noise and laughing. I didn't want to move from the couch. Even if I wanted to go home, I still had no idea how to get there, and now the trains would've stopped running.

I clutched my bag to myself and hoped Eric would return soon with my coffee.

I did parties. I did parties like nobody's business. I made chit-chat and air-kissed and I could be fun. But I didn't know parties like this. Full of strangers and conversations I had no part of. None of these people knew who I was. None of them cared.

The shrieking laughter made my head hurt. I looked around and noticed two girls glimpsing at me and laughing.

People behind me talked about things that meant nothing to me, like they spoke some kind of foreign language. I didn't have to even attempt conversation to know that this year's fashion collection would NOT be appropriate.

I searched through my bag for my phone. Not that I expected anyone to call or message me, but it would give me something to do. Maybe I should message Angie and tell her to get over here. She'd be great at a party like this, for sure. But then maybe she wasn't here for a reason. I didn't know her well enough to just casually invite her to someone else's party and, oh yeah, I didn't know the address.

"How are you feeling?"

Jack Colt put a mug of coffee on the table beside me and sat down on the other side of the couch.

"Fine. I'm totally fine," I said. I sat up straighter and pulled my dress down around my knees. I noticed I'd spilt something on it and tried to adjust myself to hide it.

He just raised an eyebrow.

I hadn't said anything stupid, had I? I wanted to tell him how great he'd been onstage and how his music made me feel. If only I could get the words together right but, before I could say anything, a guy in ripped jeans sat down on the other couch.

I picked up my coffee. Ah, coffee. My friend. Just the smell made me feel better. Then I took a sip.

Oh. My. God.

That was maybe the grossest thing I'd ever had in my mouth.

"What the hell is this?"

Maybe Jack Colt had done it on purpose. As a gag. Make the worst coffee ever, then laugh at me when I drank it.

But he wasn't laughing. Not at me. He and the other guy kept talking.

"What about that chick after the gig, mate? She wanted a piece of you."

"Her and the rest of them. It's always the same thing. 'You were so great up there. The way you played touched me deep inside. No one's made me feel like that.'"

He imitated her in a high-pitched voice.

Did guys really talk like that about women? Guys like that obviously did. What pigs. I crossed "Be nice to Jack Colt" off my mental to-do list. The bad taste in my mouth wasn't just from that disgusting coffee.

"The worst thing is, afterwards they think they own you."

"It's about the music, right?" Ripped Jeans added. "Chicks just hold you back."

I gave Ripped Jeans a sweeping look. I don't think many women would be in a hurry to hold him back. Not in that way, anyway.

"You coming?" Ripped Jeans nodded his head at a door near the kitchen. It looked like it led to the bathroom.

He got up and Jack followed him.

Whoa, he's gay? Poor Angie. She had no chance. It did explain all the misogynist chat, though. He hated woman and batted for the other team. Though no gay guy I'd ever met talked about women like that.

I curled up on the couch, hoping everyone would shut up and let me sleep.

Then it hit me. They weren't gay. The bathroom thing plus rock party. I'd seen movies. I knew what went down.

No matter how badly I needed the money, I had no intention of getting mixed up with a bunch of junkie rockers.

I marched to the bathroom, expecting to see a scene of carnage. People lolling around in a drug-crazed stupor with needles hanging out of their arms. Blank eyes and drooling mouths. Razor blades and blood, all thrown together in a gritty black-and-white montage.

But Jack couldn't be a junkie, surely. He was far too buff and meaty-looking. Junkies were pale and pathetic. Kind of like vampires without the fangs. I'm pretty sure they didn't have ripped six-packs.

I smashed the door open, ignoring the voice screaming in my head for me to stop. Nothing I saw in there would do me any good.

Someone clutched my wrist and I swung around.

"Hannah, I don't think you want to go in there." Eric looked at me with concern.

I'd seen it, though. A chick with long black hair leaning over the sink snorting something; a few others including Jack standing around. There were definitely drugs being done in there but nothing like I'd imagined. No needles. No crazy-eyed stares. No black-and-white.

Eric pulled me away.

"It's nothing, Hannah. It's just a bit of party fun. It's not like we do this every day."

I hadn't said anything, but I must have had disapproval all over my face.

"It's cool. You guys can do what you want."

I folded my arms and thought about this. Would it hurt me in any way? Like if they got busted, would it wash off on me? Could I deny all knowledge? I was only their manager. Not even a real manager, just a tentative one.

"It's just that?" I asked.

Eric nodded.

"What about you? Do you..."

Eric shrugged.

"Now and then, but it's not really my thing. But surely you've tried drugs before? I mean, everybody has."

Before I could answer, a girl ran over and threw her arms around him. In amongst the hugs and screeching, I'd been forgotten.

I leaned against the wall, trying to process this. Eric seemed like a pretty nice guy and he wasn't at all freaked out. As I looked around the room, I realised I was the only normal one here. Someone had put on a DVD and the weird music from the concert pumped through the room. It wasn't rock like Storm played and it sure as hell wasn't pop. Just seemed like a constant wailing. A couple of girls in hippy dresses danced to it, writhing like snakes, with the bracelets on their arms clattering.

And there were two guys helping themselves to food out of the fridge. Just pulling things out and making sandwiches. Even though it wasn't their house. Who does that? Had they been raised by wolves?

"Hey, it's the tortured princess."

The girl with the long black hair threw her arm around me. I hated people touching me. And why was she calling me tortured princess? Had Jack called me that? I looked around for him but couldn't see him. Maybe he was still in the bathroom. That was a nasty thing to call someone.

"Having a good time, princess?" she asked, then glanced at someone across the room and they both laughed.

"What's funny?" I asked.

But the girl kept laughing. She looked at me as though she was about to say something, then doubled over laughing again.

I squirmed out of her arms and headed to the courtyard, trying to get away from these freaks. I'd get the GPS working on my phone, then I could work out a way to get home. I sat on the wooden bench to one side, trying to get a Wi-Fi connection. I had some money in the bank. If I got a cab, I could stop at an

ATM and make a withdrawal. I'd be short on money for food for the week, but better that than suffering through this night.

The door slid open. I wasn't in the mood to socialise and I wished whoever it was would go away and leave me alone.

"Hannah. Hey, Hannah." It was Spud. I think, of the entire band, Spud hated me the most. Or maybe Jack hated me the most and Spud just copied him. I didn't even know who hated me the most. I just wanted to go home.

I got up to leave, but Spud pulled me back down on the seat.

"Don't go yet, Hannah. We need to get to know each other."

If he even thought about "getting to know each other" in any sense that involved his body coming into contact with mine, I'd kick him in the balls. This party was shit. I felt like shit. I didn't even know why I was here.

Spud didn't move any closer, though. Instead he pulled a joint out of his pocket and lit it. He took a deep drag, then handed it to me.

I waved it away.

"Oh, come on, Hannah. Don't rich girls like you do pot? You into the good stuff, huh?"

I nodded my head.

Okay, I might sound like I'm lame and all goody-two-shoes but I've never done any drugs at all. It's not a moral thing. Well, maybe it is. See, growing up, going to parties all that, I'd had one idea planted in my head.

If you do drugs, you get caught. And, if you get caught, you end up in the papers and that will cause a SCANDAL.

Of course, the "you" in that sentence wasn't a general "you" but a very specific me "you." See, when you are richer than most people, you are also of more interest than most people. So, I'd grown up thinking a scandal was the thing I had to avoid most. If you had your name in the paper, it had to be in the business section or the social section. Not the front pages.

"Come on, a tiny toke won't hurt you. Might relax you a bit. You're all tense."

I crouched on the edge of the seat, my hands fidgeting in my lap. Through the doors, I could see Jack and the black-haired girl watching me and laughing.

Screw them. Screw everyone. I took the joint from Spud and took a big drag on it.

Then I coughed. And I coughed. I thought my lungs would come up my throat and splatter all over the ground. Spud slapped me on the back.

"That's the way, Hannah."

I stood up and walked into the kitchen. I had to make my way through all those people, but my legs suddenly felt so heavy that I was aware of each movement of each step, each section of my foot rising from the ground. I had to be walking in slow motion but I focused on the kitchen.

Suddenly, everything just seemed so funny. The guy with an earring stretching a big hole in his ear. Hilarious. The girl talking in the high-pitched voice. Too funny.

The world had gone fuzzy and blurry around the edges.

I found a glass and poured myself a water and then wrapped my hands around it as though it were the most precious thing in the world. I made my way back to the couch and sat down very carefully, not wanting to spill my water.

A couple sat on the other couch drinking from teacups. As I watched them pour from the teapot, I realised it wasn't tea.

"What are you drinking?" I asked, but my voice felt thick and heavy as though it wasn't coming from me but from somewhere behind a heavy curtain.

"Wine," they answered.

And I giggled because it seemed so clever yet at the same time so pointless.

Then I noticed the cup of coffee I'd not drunk sitting on the coffee table. It stared at me with evil intent. I couldn't look at it. I had to avert my gaze. If I looked at the cup of coffee, it would know I hated it and didn't want to drink it. It would draw me in and try to doom me.

Instead I watched the lights on the DVD player. They looked so pretty. I'd never noticed how pretty lights on a DVD player were before. They spelt out words. If I kept watching them, maybe they'd spell out a message...

Eric sat down beside me. I felt like we'd merged and become one. He didn't need to speak, we didn't need words between us. We could just know each other's thoughts. He rubbed my shoulder but it wasn't like his hand and my shoulder, just an extension of each other. Joined together in this wonderful blurry haze.

"Are you okay, Hannah?" he asked.

As soon as he asked that, it all fell apart. I wasn't part of him at all. That had been a trick. He was there and I was here and my brain felt so confused. I didn't even know if I could trust him.

I tried to tell him I was fine but the words felt too thick to come out my throat so I just nodded.

"Well, if you need anything, let me know."

Then I thought about it. Why did Eric think I needed help? Maybe I didn't look fine. Maybe I looked terrible. That's why people kept staring at me. I had something wrong with me.

I should ask someone. But who could I ask?

I reached for the glass of water but my arms had been weighed down with bricks. They weren't my arms. They were someone else's. I had to think straight. I had to get back to my sane, rational sense. But all I wanted was to curl myself into a ball so no one could see me or do anything to me. When I looked up, everyone stared at me. If they didn't stare, they weren't staring on purpose.

If I didn't get out of here soon, someone would talk to me. And I couldn't let them do that. I had to move without anyone noticing.

There were steps going up to a loft. If I could get up there, I'd be safe. But how could I do that without anyone noticing?

Then the doorbell rang. It was the police. Oh my god, what could I do? I'd be busted. I knew this would happen. I just knew it. I had to get away.

Nobody seemed to panic but I had a moment of clarity. I was the only one who could sense this impending doom. I couldn't warn them, I just had to save myself.

My heart pounded crazy fast. It drowned out the music and the talk. All I could hear was my heart. People had to be looking at me. They had to be able to hear it too.

If I ran, it'd only draw attention to me. If I sat here, I'd get busted. Then everyone seemed to herd around the doorway so I took my chance and bolted for the stairs.

As I reached the top, I smelt pizza. It smelt so good. I wanted nothing more than a slice of pizza. I didn't eat pizza but right now, I'd kill a man for a slice. There was one thing I wanted more, though, and that was to be alone.

I opened the door to one of the rooms but didn't turn on the light. If I turned on the light, people would know I was there and they'd come for me. The police downstairs, the pizza police, they'd know.

I fumbled around until I found the wardrobe. I opened the door and felt something warm and comforting. A lambswool jacket. Perfect. It would protect me from the pizza police. I put it on, then kicked the shoes on the bottom of the wardrobe into a pile and curled myself into a corner, well hidden behind the clothes. The door wouldn't close properly so I tried to pile the shoes around me to form a barricade.

I must have fallen asleep for a while because the next thing I knew light filtered in through the crack in the wardrobe door and I could hear people moving. They couldn't find me in here, not with the jacket wrapped around me. I'd just stay really quiet and they'd go away.

Bedsprings creaked like someone had sat down on them and I heard muffled voices and a moan. These people weren't looking for me; they were up to something else entirely.

I had to get out of here but, if I left the wardrobe, they'd see me. The moans increased and I knew I was trapped.

Then I heard a zipper.

Followed by slurping sounds. Oh. My. God. No. Not that. I pulled the collar of the jacket up over my ears, hoping to block out the sound. Maybe they'd be finished soon. It helped, until the voice started. The unmistakable voice of Jack Colt muttering, "Yeah, babe... oh yeah..."

My stomach lurched like something lived inside it. It was like I'd gotten stuck inside a bad porno. Yet, despite myself, I could feel a stirring inside me. Heat rising between my legs. Part of me wanted to move so I could see through the crack in the door but I didn't want to make a noise. My nipples hardened against the fabric of my bra and I squirmed in discomfort as the timbre of his voice deepened.

This was all a dream. It was part of the drugs and the booze. I could just ignore it and it'd go away. But the squeak of the bedsprings got louder and the sharp deep breaths and that obscene slurping.

My stomach lurched again. As I struggled to stop the part of my brain that wanted to enjoy this, it made the nausea rise in me. My belly contracted harder and that horrible choking feeling started in my throat. I tried to hold it back but there was no stopping it. Luckily, I had a bucket nearby. The rush of booze shot out of me and into that container. As I hugged it tight, someone screamed and the wardrobe door burst open. That's when I realised it wasn't a bucket but a cowboy boot. And then everything went black.

Chapter 7

When I woke up the next morning, I had no idea where I was. The sun streamed in the window, breaking my head in two. If I put my head back under the covers, it would all go away. I grabbed the pillow and put my head under the blanket. It smelt good. Lemony and spicy. I could stay there in that lemony, spicy cocoon forever and I'd not have to face anything.

I could hear banging from somewhere out there, like someone cooking. I wanted a glass of water but I couldn't think of a way of getting it without anyone seeing me. Bits of the night before raced back into my head, although I tried to push them away.

I edged my foot out of the bed, then realised I was naked.

What the hell had happened? I'd passed out and now I was naked? And where were my clothes? I'd be a prisoner in this room until someone came to dress me. Maybe that was their plan – they'd plied me with alcohol and drugs, then taken advantage of me and maybe intended holding me to ransom or least trying to get out of the contract. It hurt my head just to think about that.

Then I heard a knock at the door.

Was there anywhere in the room I could hide? The wardrobe. No. Not the wardrobe.

"Want a cup of tea?"

It was Eric.

"I guess." I couldn't hide there forever and I'd rather face Eric than Jack Colt any time. I pulled the sheet up tight under my chin but heard him walk away.

I sat up and arranged the blanket to make sure I was fully covered. My eyes had de-blurred enough so that I could focus on my surroundings. Rock posters covered the walls, a few of them curling off at the edges where they'd started to unstick. A bunch of guitar magazines and old pizza boxes surrounded the bed. Clothes piled out of the wardrobe onto the floor, mostly t-shirts and jeans but I could see an expensive-looking leather jacket hanging up, and those biker boots didn't come cheap either. I assumed this was Eric's room since he was the one making tea, but that didn't seem like the sort of stuff he'd have lying around. And somehow, he seemed like he'd be much neater.

Eric knocked again and walked in with the tea.

"Wow, you look... well, you'll feel better after this."

He sat on the edge of my bed.

"Umm, Eric... do you know where my clothes are?" I kind of choked the words out. Is there any classy or elegant way to ask where your clothes have disappeared to after a night of drinking? If there is, I don't know it.

"I'll bring them up for you. They are in the dryer. You kinda... well, you were sick last night..."

"You put my dress in the dryer?" I jumped, then realised my boob was showing. I quickly pulled up the blanket. "That dress is dry clean only. It's pure linen. It'll be wrecked."

"I'm sorry. I thought it'd be best to wash it straight away..." Eric covered his mouth and looked so upset, of course I couldn't be angry.

"That's okay. You didn't know. And at least it's clean now, right? I need something to wear home."

Eric smiled.

"Did I really throw up? That's so gross." I picked up my cup and sipped the tea.

He nodded.

"On myself? Please tell me it was just on myself and that I didn't throw up everywhere. Oh god."

He didn't meet my eyes. I'd obviously made a big vomitty mess and he'd had to clean it up. Then I remembered. The boot. Oh, hell no.

"I'm so sorry. You must hate me. And you even put me to bed after that and let me sleep here."

"It's not my bed. And it wasn't me..."

I'd meant to act like a dingbat, not a teenage girl on her first bender. Before I could say any more, someone bashed roughly on the door.

"Is she out of there yet? I need to get my gear."

Jack Colt.

He walked into the room and threw my clothes on the bed.

"Hurry up and get out. You must have things to organise – like a gig at the Metropolis."

I stared at my teacup. I really hoped that somewhere, in amongst those leaves, was a shred of my dignity that I could reclaim. I couldn't find it.

Jack grabbed some papers from the desk and walked out without a glimpse at me. I gulped down the tea.

"I'll leave you to get dressed," said Eric, standing up.

When he'd gone, I gingerly got out of bed. One foot out and then the other. I hadn't asked him who'd undressed me but if Jack Colt had carried me up there, he'd seen enough. I wanted to die. Throwing myself in the bay with rocks tied to my feet seemed like a great idea.

I put on my lingerie, which had survived the washing process intact, then looked at my dress.

The red fabric had turned motley shades of pink, like some cheap hippy tie-dye. Still, it would cover me until I got home. I pulled it over my head but it got stuck. Either I'd put on a stack of weight overnight or the dress had shrunk. Did I mention this dress had cost a small fortune? I didn't want to say anything. I didn't want Eric to feel bad but I could not leave the house wearing that dress. I needed to do something.

I found a t-shirt on the floor that at least covered my knickers. That would do so I could get downstairs and ask Eric for a loan of something to wear home. I dunno what but he was pretty skinny. Maybe he had a pair of jeans that I could tighten with a belt.

Black Sabbath, it said across the t-shirt, whoever they were.

I stumbled downstairs to the lounge room I vaguely remembered.

Eric sat at the table working on his laptop while Jack Colt sprawled on the couch strumming his guitar.

I expected the place to be a mess after the party, but you'd not have noticed that people had been there. Not even a stray glass lying around. No wondered I'd heard noise from the kitchen. Eric must have worked his butt off cleaning this place.

The place had an industrial charm but it was freezing cold. Didn't they have central heating? I stood in the middle of the room, shivering, about to ask for something else to put on.

"My Sabbath shirt? Get it off! Now!"

"I had nothing else to wear. My dress shrunk." I pulled at the hem of the t-shirt, trying to cover more of myself while Jack Colt's glare burnt through my skin.

"I don't care. Take it off."

"I'm sure as hell not stripping off here."

He went back to strumming the guitar. "Well, it's not like we haven't seen it already."

I ran back up to the bedroom and threw myself on the bed. Maybe the dress would go on if I tried really hard? I pulled it over my head and wiggled myself but could not even get it over my shoulders.

"Are you okay? I brought you up some other clothes." Eric came in with a bundle in his hands. He held up a dress. A totally shabby dress – black stretch fabric, giving the image of a cheap whore.

"Thanks, that'll be fine." Beggars can't be choosers and I needed to leave. I didn't even want to think why he had a slut dress just hanging around the house. No doubt from a floozy that Jack Colt had hanging around. They probably had a store of underwear and all kinds of things.

I stripped off the t-shirt and pulled on the dress. It seemed a bit baggy around the boobs and I wished I had a jacket or something to put over it. I looked for my shoes but they must've been downstairs, and I wished I had something to tie my hair back with.

When I got downstairs again, Jack Colt had gone. Eric drew me a map showing how to get to the train station, complete with directions. He was such a sweet guy. I didn't want to mention that the cheap polyester of the dress was giving me hives or that it crept up at the back but, before I left, he told me to wait a minute and grabbed me a jacket to wear so I didn't get cold.

On the way to the station, I grabbed a coffee, then remembered I had to pay rent. I went to the ATM and got the last five hundred dollars from my bank account. Angie had said we had work today and that Friday was payday. It wouldn't be much but it'd be something to add to the stash. Some weeks, she'd said, you get a few full days and it made for a decent pay cheque, but sometimes it was just a few hours. Maybe an extra fifty dollars or so.

I put the money in my purse and looked longingly at the pastries in a bakery window before I got to the station.

Once I got on the train, I felt sleepy. Since it was after rush hour, the carriage was half-empty and I had the seat to myself. It actually wasn't that far from Eric and Jack's place to mine, Eric had explained, but, because of the way the trains worked, I needed to go right into the city and back out again. I hated public transport. I hated that smell that sunk into the seats from thousands of unwashed butts. I hated the glare of the sun coming in the windows that you couldn't escape and the noise hissing out of a hundred iPods with cheap headphones. A couple of gangly teenagers swung from the rail on the roof of the train, their pants hung down showing their knickers, and an old man gave me sleazy looks.

I fished my sunglasses out of my bag.

Before we got to the next station, I'd dozed off.

Still half-asleep, I noticed a woman hovering over me. She had lanky hair hanging down in her face and the smell of sweat radiated off her in waves. She grinned at me, showing a few missing teeth.

"Oi, love, is this your stop?"

I jumped up. I hadn't even noticed the train had stopped in the city.

"Thanks," I called to the woman as I ran off the train. Lucky she'd woken me.

I ran to the next platform and jumped on another train. It was only a few more stops and at least I'd be home and could change into something decent.

When I got to my station, I waved my bag over the barrier gates. I had my transport card in my bag and that should've been enough to swipe it but the bloody barriers didn't open. I sighed, then fished in my bag for my wallet so I could get my card out.

My wallet wasn't there.

What the hell! It had to be. I'd put it back in my bag after I went to the ATM. I patted myself down in case I'd put it in a pocket – even though I had no pockets in my outfit. I searched again, pulling everything out of my bag to make sure. It had to be in there, but a hard lump of sick feeling settled in my stomach. Maybe it'd fallen out on the train.

I ran back to the platform but the train was long gone so I stamped my feet and looked for a staff member.

"Well, I can let you out this time but, love, if the inspectors were here, they'd bust you for sure." He looked me up and down and looked at the clock, giving me a cheeky grin. "You sure had a big night, didn't you?"

"I'm not fare evading. My wallet was stolen. And I don't want you to just let me through the barrier, I want you to contact a station down the line so they can check the train for my wallet."

The train guy rolled his eyes.

"They can't do that. Most of the stations further down the line aren't even manned. Best you'll get is maybe some kind person will hand your wallet in. You can call the central lost and found tomorrow."

"But my money..."

"Reckon that's long gone. You didn't notice anything drop out of your bag?"

"No. I had it right on the seat beside me the whole time. Unless it dropped out when that woman woke me up."

He shook his head. "Are you stupid? You were asleep and some woman woke you up? Didn't you check then? What are you, five years old? Wouldn't the first thing you did be check your bag?"

"I had to run to catch the other train."

He shook his head some more. "A fool and his money are soon parted. That's what my Nan always said. But here, I'll give you the number to call, just in case. You might get your cards and stuff back. Don't tell me you had other valuables in there? Cancel your credit cards straightaway. You could go to the police but I doubt they'd be able to do much."

The bank had already cancelled my credit cards. I only had that cash. And maybe three dollars or so in change in the bottom of my bag.

I wanted to scream. I wanted to punch something. Why couldn't the police do anything? I'd seen the woman, I'd be able to identify her. They could drag people in and I'd pick her out of a line-up. I kicked the wall on my way out. I kicked it hard.

Stupid trains. Stupid train people. But it didn't make me feel better. It just hurt my foot.

I called in at the local police station on my way home but all they did was make me fill in some paperwork and, like the guy at the station, they told me I should be more careful in future. I didn't think that was a very good way to protect the safety and property of the general public, but the police officer just said they were understaffed and they couldn't run after every thief who took an opportunity.

That meant I had fifty dollars in wages due to me, and – well, nothing. A possibility of some money from the band in the future but nothing at all concrete. I had rent due at the end of the week and, if I didn't pay, I'd be out on the street. I could make sure I wasn't home when they came around. Yeah, they collected my rent in cash. Nothing dodgy about that, nothing dodgy at all. But, even if I avoided them, sooner or later, I'd have to pay or they might chuck my stuff out.

I sighed. When Dad had told me I had to be tough, I don't think he realised how tough I needed to be. Where was he? I'd done enough. I'd learnt all my lessons. Surely it was time this finished.

If I contacted Tom for a loan, he'd ask a lot of questions. I guess I could call Frank, but really he'd been a bit creepy and weird since this had happened, as though it gave him some kind of sick pleasure seeing me down and out. And I'd get another lecture about being stupid for having my wallet stolen. Nobody tells you about things before they happen but afterwards everyone's an expert.

I'd have bought one of those delish pastries if I'd known some scumbag was going to steal my money anyway. There was no point in even trying not to spend money in this world. Fate just stepped in and punished you.

Anyway, I could deal with this myself. I was strong. I just had to use my brain and my initiative and put myself into "poor person" mode. I bet poor people dealt with this kind of thing all the time and I was obviously smarter than them.

When I got home, I threw myself on the bed. I'd just sleep for the next few days until Friday, then I'd not have to eat or do anything that cost money. That would be for the best. Except I had to book the band into that club and I had to come up with a grand for the video cost. My stomach rumbled and I realised I'd had nothing but a cup of tea all day.

I emptied out my bag and counted my change. I had $3.15. That wouldn't even buy a burger. My stomach rumbled louder. Then I remembered the box in the cupboard. Filled with chocolate tree frogs. I opened the packet and took a bite. Then nearly spat it out. I checked the packaging again. These things were organic, sugar-free chocolate. The 'guilt-free' treat. Guilt-free, my butt. They should feel guilty for even making these nasty things. And I should feel guilty for handing them out to unsuspecting people.

I finished eating it, though, because food is food.

Then I spent a long time lying on my bed, looking at the cracks in the ceiling. When you have a problem, cracks in the ceiling are probably the worst advisors to turn to for answers, but I had nothing else. The white ceiling had water stains that looked like deformed zoo animals and the cracks were like the fences holding them in. If it wasn't for those cracks, the water stain animals would surely get free and attack me.

Then I jumped up. I had an idea. What had I been thinking? I was sitting on a gold mine. Almost literally. All my money problems would be over.

Chapter 8

"I only do commission sales," the girl said, twirling her hair around her finger, but she had the hunger in her eyes. I recognised it.

"Yeah? Well, I need the money now."

I figured if I just stood there until she said yes, she'd give in eventually. I hadn't lugged two huge bags of clothes all the way across town, using my last coins on train fare, to sell stuff on commission. She was getting a super bargain and she knew it. There were thousands of dollars of designer clothes in those bags. Not to mention handbags and shoes.

I'd sorted through the clothes in my room, ruthlessly putting them into piles of things I could sell. I'd made myself have a heart of stone. Absolute stone. No emotion at all. That formal gown I'd worn when Tom first kissed me – gone. The shoes I'd worn to my debutante ball – gone. The fabulous one-off gown that made me look as if I was made of diamonds – didn't need it.

When I picked up the fab Valentino boots I'd only bought a few months ago and never worn, I started to falter.

"Heart of stone, Hannah," I reminded myself and put them in the "for sale" pile.

I looked at what was left. A couple of Donna Karan dresses for those power bitch meetings, a few pairs of jeans and some t-shirts, my leather jacket that had a price tag so high I could've bought a small apartment for the same price and some cute dresses.

I picked up the top I'd worn the night I'd gone to see Storm play, about to toss it in the bag, but, for some stupid reason, I lifted it to my face and sniffed it. Something about the smell made me happy for a moment. I decided to keep it. With all the beer stains and muck on it, I doubted it would sell anyway.

"Heart of stone," I told myself again and remembered that someone had told me it was character building to help the unfortunate. Who is more unfortunate than those who have to buy second-hand clothes? It wasn't as if I was losing my clothes anyway. I was just clearing out my wardrobe so I could replace things in the future. I had nowhere to wear this stuff and it'd all get ruined and be unwearable and worthless soon.

"Why are you selling all this stuff, anyway?" the shopgirl asked.

"I lost weight and don't need them any more." Like I'd tell her I needed the money or I'd starve to death. "I don't want the hassle of having to come back here, so just give me some cash and it's a done deal. There's other shops, you know."

I put my hands on my hips and stared her down.

She sighed. "Yes, and they work on a commission basis too."

"Not for good-quality stuff like this. You know you want it."

I took a top out of the bag. Still this season's fashion. That'd be snapped up in no time.

She picked up a calculator and tapped in a number, then held it up to show me. It was way, way less than those clothes were worth, even second-hand, and she knew it.

I hesitated, then picked up the calculator and tapped in a number myself. She shook her head. We locked eyes, both not wanting to back down. Then my stomach rumbled again and I just couldn't stand the thought of another of those bloody fake chocolate tree frogs. I tapped in another number and she nodded. Score, I'd get cash.

As she handed me the invoice to sign, I nearly cried. Those clothes were my friends and now I was selling them for some cold, hard cash. What kind of monster would sell their friends for cash? A hungry monster that got rolled on the train, I guess. I took a moment to say a silent goodbye to all those darling little shoes and those sweet twin sets. No mother sending her kids off to school for the first time would ever have felt so bad. But then I guess a mother doesn't have to worry about her kids being stretched over the girth of some fat chick's belly in a change room. On the other hand, I could buy new, better clothes one day but she's stuck with the same crummy kids.

Heart of stone.

She handed me the bundle of cash and I put it in my bag, then realised that wasn't safe. I spied a cheap wallet in the display case.

"How about you throw that in for free?"

"It's a hundred bucks."

"Like hell it is. It's a fake. The logo is even a little bit off in the printing. You can't sell a fake for that much. Come on, you *are* making a bundle here."

She sighed and handed me the wallet.

I grinned. The wallet totally *wasn't* a fake but she'd fallen for it. See, when you look classy, you get away with murder.

I had enough money for rent and for the video costs and to buy myself a delicious burger for dinner. Today was really looking up. I went to the café where I'd gone the other day. The one with the hanging ferns. I ordered coffee and my burger, then decided to move to Step 2 of the Get Hannah Out of Poverty Plan.

I took a deep breath and made the call. I put on my best business voice and asked about getting a booking.

"Sorry, we aren't booking new bands at the moment."

"But you're a band booker. That's what you do. And this band is hot. They are like the biggest band around at the moment. I can send you their demo."

I tapped my fingers on the table. Was this some crap he gave to everyone to see if they were determined? Well, I was determined. I was more determined than them all.

"Fifty times a day, I hear from bands that are the hottest thing around or the next big thing. They all want the same thing but we're booked solid for the next month. Maybe longer. I have enough bands that can drag in a crowd knocking at my door, I don't need to take a chance on an unknown."

"Well, they are hardly unknown."

"Unless they can pull in over five thousand people guaranteed, they're unknown to me."

I quickly calculated the crowd at that bar the other night. I'm pretty sure it was less than five thousand. A lot less.

"I'll just send you the demo—"

"I don't need it. I've got to go. I'm busy."

"You'll regret that."

"Maybe I will. Maybe I won't. I'll take that chance. Now, goodbye."

Argghhh, what a pig. I could see him sitting there, stroking his big belly while smoking a cigar. Didn't he realise how important this was to me? I had a feeling "I tried my best" wouldn't cut it with Jack Colt. If they had walked away at that meeting, I couldn't stop them, but if they acknowledged me as their manager, I could get my cut of the band money and maybe sell the management company for a decent amount.

Why did I think I could do this? I didn't know the first thing about managing a band. Who knew you could ring up to make a booking and be told no? It seemed wrong, like they should at least listen to the demo first and see if the band was any good. Anyone would think they just cared about making money and nothing else.

I thought about my options. I could get a job. A real job. I didn't know what I could do since I'd dropped out of my degree. I could maybe be a secretary or a waitress. Probably not even that. I had no experience. No skills. Well, apart from ballet lessons and being able to ride a pony and talking French. They didn't seem like very handy skills, though.

My only hope was for Dad to come back and I hadn't even heard from him once.

I swirled the spoon in my coffee.

"Hey, there."

Angie sat down opposite me.

"I've got the money for the video," I told her. "But I don't think the band is going to agree."

I explained to her about the deal and how I had to get them booked at the Metropolis. How I'd tried and how I'd miserably failed.

"Well, I wouldn't think five thousand people would be that hard. I can start a mailing list on the website and see how many numbers I get."

"Yeah, we could just invite Jack Colt's ex-girlfriends."

I grinned, but I wasn't sure if she could get five thousand people. It seemed impossible and she hadn't heard how rude that guy was on the phone. Once, I'd have just got my dad to call back and make him an offer he couldn't refuse, but those days were gone. Things were really tough for the ordinary people.

"We just need a plan."

"I don't know about plans... I'm not even cut out for this job."

Then I broke down and told her all about what happened the day before. All the gory details.

"Oh, you bitch, I hate you," she said with a grin, so I knew she didn't mean it.

"Why? I made a complete idiot of myself."

"Yeah, but you're hot and classy. That's a winning combination, right. I have no chance at all with Jack Colt with you around."

"I'm not so hot. Look at my hair. It's in urgent need of a cut. My eyelashes need redoing. And look at this manicure!"

"You are going to steal his heart and I won't even get my two weeks."

"I don't want his heart. You can keep it. What about Eric? He's a sweet guy." I did feel a bit of a tingle, though. Not that I wanted a chance with Jack Colt but I'd like to think that if I wanted to, I could. I could not work out that kiss. Maybe I'd just dreamt it. Dreamt that before I'd gone to sleep in my trashed state, someone had leaned over the bed and kissed me. But sometimes it was like I could still feel the ghost of his lips on my forehead.

She picked at her nails. "He's nice but not my type." Then she looked at me carefully. "Do you like Eric? You do, don't you? Oh, you'd make such a cute couple. And that would leave Jack for me."

"I don't want Jack and I don't want Eric. I have a boyfriend. Tom. He's away at school."

And I hadn't even remembered to call him. Yikes. Who forgets their own boyfriend? But then, what could I say if I did call? That I'd had to sell my clothes to make rent money and I'd had to take on managing a rock band, only to get drunk and stoned and end up naked and sleeping at their apartment. My life hadn't been that much to brag about lately. If Tom knew how broke I was, he'd drop me like a rock. I was the trophy girlfriend with the perfect life and he was the trophy boyfriend. Now I was a trophy with battered sides.

"Do you have a photo?"

I reached into my bag, then remembered it was in my stolen wallet. Shit, soon I wouldn't even remember what Tom looked like. I'd get back to school and not even know my own boyfriend. He'd blend into every other guy in our group with their plans for shining careers, their European holidays in summer and ski trips in winter, their latest cars and their latest phones.

Not that I was all that fond of being poor or anything, but that life started to look a little bit boring. I couldn't remember any time in that life I'd felt as exhilarated as I did bartering that woman up to an extra five hundred dollars for a pile of my old clothes.

"So what are you up to tonight? If you want, you can come over to my place. We'll get a bottle of wine and maybe listen to those Storm demos and think up a plan for getting the gig. Look, the dude has to book bands, right? Otherwise there'd be no one playing there. So, all we have to do is work out how everyone else does it, then do it even better. Plus, I'll give you a manicure."

"Sounds good to me." I don't know why but the way Angie said this and the way she grinned made me think it was a real possibility. A glimmer of hope returned to my heart.

We walked to her place, passed the little cafés and shops selling clothes by local designers. Some of the outfits on display were kinda cute, and not all that expensive either. Just imagine, me wearing clothes by an unknown designer. I thought I could make that work. It might even be doing the designer a favour.

Then Angie nudged me.

"Jack. Jack Colt. Over there."

I looked across the street and saw him, running after a woman. The woman wore a super short skirt and high heels she could barely walk in. Even from this distance, she looked a fair bit older than him but like she worked really hard to hide it. From her outfit, I wondered if she was the one that had left the dress at his place. It was cheap and slutty, just the same. Maybe he had a secret girlfriend. Why did that thought make my belly hurt? I didn't care about Jack Colt, not one little bit.

Then he caught up with her and grabbed her hand and thrust some money into it. She turned and threw her arms around his neck.

"Erk, looks like neither of us have a chance with him."

"She's welcome to him." I didn't care who he hung around with. It meant nothing to me.

"Did you see her? She looked nearly old enough to be his mother."

I turned back to take another glance.

"Maybe not mother. Maybe mother's younger sister?"

She'd slipped his arm around his waist as they walked off down the street together. If he had to hang around with his floozies, he could at least do it in his own neighbourhood, not mine.

Chapter 9

So, the next morning we were in tree frog outfits again and working the train station. A different station this time but the same drill. Two hours and then we could ditch these stupid costumes and work on Plan B.

Angie had decided that we had to make Storm look big, really big. We had to plaster posters all around the Metropolis building so that was all the booker would see when he left. We would walk up and down playing Storm loudly. We'd stalk the staff when they left for lunch and talk really loudly about how much we loved the Storm gig and what a great band they were. It seemed a bit of a dodgy scheme, but what did I know? At least it sounded better than some of her other plans, like breaking into his office and changing his ringtone on his phone to a Storm song, then ringing him constantly until he got the song stuck in his head.

"You've gotta be a bit more bouncy," Angie told me. "You can't scowl at people. You'll scare them off. No one likes a snarky tree frog."

"Like hell they don't. They're grabbing these free frog chocolates like they haven't seen food for a year. What's the problem with people? Most of them don't even say thank you. You'd think they were brought up by wolves or something." I saw another hand shoot out for a free sample. "Hey, kid, no more for you. I've seen you walk past here like five times. You've scored enough freebies."

"Hold on, here comes another surge of them."

The commuters herded down the stairs to the concourse in a huge wave. Most of them dressed in navy or black with sour expressions on their faces, as the sound of their stomping footsteps echoed around me. I tried putting a sincere-looking smile on my face but, to be honest, it was a bit scary having them all approach like that, then rip the free chocolates out of my hand before I even had a chance to hand them out. I reached into my bag to refill and a woman yelled at me for being too slow. As if she was entitled to my freebies. I'd have snapped back at her but remembered I needed the money. I really needed the money. Even though the pay was shit, that extra bit I'd earn meant the difference between sleeping at night and being kept awake wondering what I'd do if things hadn't improved by the time my paltry savings ran out. Anyway, once she tasted those chocolate tree frogs, revenge would be mine.

I filled up the dinky little cane basket I had over my hands and stood up.

"Hannah! Is that really you? What the hell are you doing?"

The chick in front of me in her tailored suit gave me the once-over, then wrinkled her nose as though something smelt bad. I recognised her. We'd gone to school together but I didn't remember her name.

I turned my face, hoping she'd get the hint and go away. I could run for an exit before... wait, she'd said my name. She'd already recognised me. There was no escape.

"Oh my god, what's happened to you?" she shrieked, so that everyone across the station could hear. "I'd heard rumours about your dad but didn't realise it'd come to this. Oh, you poor thing."

She rubbed my arm. I grimaced and handed her a tree frog.

"I'm doing this for charity. For the sick children." I wasn't sure if she believed me but it sounded plausible.

As she walked off, I saw her get her phone out of her bag. No doubt to ring everyone she'd ever met to tell them.

When our shift was over, we stuffed our tree frog costumes and all the posters and a few rolls of tape into a bag, and headed across town.

When we got there, we couldn't believe it. There were already three different lots of people sticking up posters. The construction site opposite the venue had a wall filled with posters but we started sticking ours up over them. As soon as we'd put one up, someone covered it with theirs. It looked like every band in town had the same idea and most of them had better posters. Posters with coloured printing on glossy paper. We just had cheap photocopies. How can you look like a promising up-and-coming band with black-and-white posters?

"Hey, get away, that's our spot," Angie shouted and chased a nerdy guy off down the street, but he'd be back as soon as she turned around.

"It looks like a lot of other people have the same idea."

Down the street, music blasted out of an old ghetto blaster while some guys drove around in a beat-up car playing more loud music out of their stereo.

I squatted down on the street.

"I don't think this will work." It started to dawn on me. There were probably a thousand or more bands in this town that were just as keen as we were. And that was just to play at this one place. Even if the band played there, it'd just be one night. Being an overnight success took a lot of work. Luckily, I had something a bit more devious planned.

Angie squatted beside me and lit up a cigarette.

"None of them have the nous to do our lunch stalking plan, though," she whispered to me.

"How will we know what he looks like when he does leave?"

"I got a pic of him off the Internet. I searched his name and there he was at some record launch party. You'll recognise him. He's got a massive nose. You'll see his nose leave the building before he does. Oi, you, get away from our posters."

Angie ran down the street after the guy. She came panting back.

"I shouldn't run with a cigarette in my mouth. Argghh, my lungs are burning."

"What's so good about playing here, anyway?" I looked up at the big white building with its Gothic architecture. It looked a bit old and crumbling to me. The front was covered in posters for bands but the office was around the side with a crappy little doorway leading onto the street.

"It's one of the biggest venues in town and lots of record company knobs show up to watch bands. You have to be able to pack in five thousand people just to get a support gig, right, so that's a helluva lot of people for a headliner. It makes you look like you're really hot."

"Hey, is that him?" Perfect timing for my secret plan.

"Yeah, come on. Just leave all that poster shit here."

We took off down the street after him but he walked at a brisk pace. He was a skinny dude, not fat like I'd imagined, and he wore a long overcoat even though the day was sunny. He headed into a little café and ordered lunch, then went to sit in the courtyard out the back.

We ordered coffees, then followed him out the back.

Angie was right. No one else had followed. Those guys were all too busy with their poster wars to even think of stalking like we'd done.

Angie sat down and launched into a dialogue about the gig the other night. How it'd been so crowded and she thought she'd be turned away at the door, how fantastic their set had been, how much she was looking forward to seeing them next time.

"Jack Colt of Storm is seriously the best. He's so charismatic, people just flock to see him. I think Storm are going to be huge. They are so different to all those other bands." Subtlety wasn't Angie's strong point.

He spun around and stared at us.

"So, which one of you is their manager?"

I nodded.

"Do you know how many times a week I have to sit here and listen to someone banging on about their band while I try to enjoy my lunch?"

I tried to grin, a lopsided, embarrassed grin. But really, why take on the job if he didn't like being bugged about bands?

He walked over to our table, looked Angie over, then turned as if to dismiss her. He then looked at me. I wore a tight t-shirt and a cute little skirt. I'd needed something fairly tight so it fit under that stupid tree frog costume. His eyes moved down to my cleavage and stayed there. Seriously, like his eyeballs had fallen out and nested between my boobs.

He didn't speak for a minute, long enough to creep me out. I adjusted the neckline of my t-shirt but it didn't seem to help. He was creepy and gross, standing over me like that. I wondered if I should stand up.

Before I could move, his hand reached out to stroke my arm. I turned to get away from him but he kept patting me.

"Maybe, if you can be really nice, I might find an opening..."

My mouth dropped open. Was he saying what I thought he was saying? Gross. I wanted them to get this gig, but not that much. Hells, if I was going to go to that extreme, I could just become a hooker and be done with it. I wanted to respond but my mouth just opened and closed like a goldfish out of water. That wasn't part of my plan at all.

"Like hell she'll be *nice*. You piece of shit. Come on, Hannah, let's get out of here. It's starting to stink."

Angie had jumped up from her seat and grabbed my hand.

I followed her out and almost ran into someone coming the other way. I looked up to see a familiar face.

"Frank, how are you going?"

"Hannah!" He kissed my cheek.

"Good to see you looking so well."

"Yeah, I've taken over the management business. Just doing some work at the moment. How totally unexpected to see you here."

"Ha, always said you were the brains in the family." He patted my arm. "Come over for dinner one night. Hey, you should meet Jason. I'm having lunch with him and he's worth knowing if you want to get some band business done." He looked over at the sleazeball.

"Come and join us." The sleazeball was all smiles for us now that Frank was here.

"Sorry, I've got to run." Angie took my hand and pulled me away. I probably shouldn't have brought her here with me. She'd mess this up.

As I said that, the waitress turned up with our coffees. "Where are you sitting, girls?"

Frank nodded to Jason's table and we sat down.

"Have you met Hannah?" he asked the sleaze. "She's practically like a daughter to me. And this is..." Frank turned to Angie.

"Angie, our social media manager."

"Yes, we've met. I think we had a bit of a misunderstanding. I was making a little joke and she took it the wrong way."

Angie kicked my foot under the table. There was no misunderstanding. You don't mistake a leer.

"Hannah is working in band management now. For Megastar Management."

"Are they still around? I thought the company folded years ago."

Well, that was really tactful of him. Still, he'd recognised the name. I'd not even thought of using it when I called, figuring it'd mean nothing.

"I'm sure you could really help her out," added Frank. "She's sure to have some bands you could put on your schedule."

"Yes, we'd been talking about one of them. What were they called? Stork?"

"Storm," I said. I bit my lip and didn't meet his eyes. "I have their demo in my bag."

"That's okay. If they are with Megastar Management I'm sure we can find a spot for them." Sleazy Jason gave Frank a smile, like a dog wanting a reward for doing a trick. He took out his phone and flicked through it. "Ah, we've had a band cancel for next Tuesday. Do you think they could fill in then?"

I nodded.

"Wow, Hannah," said Frank. "I'll be there. I'd like to see you in manager mode with this band."

Frank winked at me. He was the best. I'd have totally got up and kissed him if I could've. Jason gulped, knowing he was fully committed to having the band play now. With Frank turning up, he'd have to keep his word.

It'd worked out just as Frank had said it would when I'd called him the other night. We'd not even had to work the sexual harassment angle. I'd just had to act gullible and let Frank do the rest. Angie had helped too in her own way. Still, I could've done with less of that Jason creep.

Jason told me the details and said he'd follow up with an email.

"Okay, we've finished our coffee. Nice meeting you, Jason." There may have been a touch of sarcasm in my tone but just a touch. "And see you on Tuesday, Frank."

We didn't whoop until we got well clear of the café. Then Angie grabbed my hands and swung me around. She even did a little dance on the street.

"You are officially, acceptably the manager now."

"Is it okay doing things like that? It's not like I used my own ability or anything?"

Angie elbowed me hard in the ribs.

"You are kidding, right? It's who you know in this business. And you know some hotshot lawyer, which is totes awesome. Hey, am I really the social media manager? That's sweet as. I need to get business cards printed."

She was right. I'd be totally accepted as manager now but I had a bit of a sick feeling in my belly, having to work with that sleazebag.

Chapter 10

I couldn't wait to see the look on Jack Colt's face when I told him I'd booked the gig. It'd be like I was fully vindicated. I'd be the one who got them the gig at the Metropolis, not the girl who'd thrown up in his cowboy boots while some chick gave him head... I figured I should go around and tell them straightaway and maybe, while I was there, get a contact number for them. It wasn't as if I wanted to see him or anything.

I knocked at the door of the apartment, hoping they were home. I looked around while I waited now that I had non-blurry eyes to see out of. For all this place looked so grungy, it couldn't be that cheap. It wasn't cheap grungy. It was like industrial chic grunge. And it wasn't just an apartment like I'd first thought either but the whole building. I could hear music coming from inside, so I knew they were home.

Maybe one of them had rich parents. I had no idea what Jack did for money outside the band and Spud apparently lived in the outer suburbs with his parents.

The door was opened by a tiny Asian woman, who I assumed was Eric's mother.

She put her hands on her hips and examined me.

"Who are you?"

"I'm Hannah. I'm the manager."

"Ah, Hannah, come in. Eric told me about you. I'm just making dinner for him. He doesn't eat enough. But this band, it's not such a good idea. He's not going to make money from that. He should go back to study and become a lawyer. Or, if he's going to do music, he should do some nice pop music like those boys from Big Bang."

I had no idea who Big Bang were but Eric-Mama didn't need any reaction from me. She hurried inside and I could smell something that smelt like awesome in smell form. If Eric-Mama was cooking I was so planning to stick around for dinner.

"Are Eric and Jack home?"

"Jack! Eric! Hannah is here."

Eric came out of his room.

"Hannah, hey, I'll get Jack."

They both came downstairs.

"I've got brilliant news," I said. "I've booked the Metropolis. Next Tuesday night."

I grinned at Jack Colt with a big shit-eating grin. Ha. He thought I couldn't do it.

"Fine. Is that all you had to say? Because I'm in the middle of something."

He turned to walk back up the stairs.

"Yes. That's all I've got to say. And you could say a bit more. Maybe thank you or something like that would be nice. You wanted to play there and I booked it. So suck it up and get ready for your career to begin."

He shrugged. I wanted to hit him. I wanted to hit him so bad. My eyeballs would surely pop out of my head from the pressure building up. The ungrateful bastard. I thought about throwing something at him but Eric-Mama caught my eye. Something about her made me want to create a good impression, so I just silently fumed instead.

"That's fantastic, Hannah. I can't believe you managed it, and for so soon too. We need to get posters done and to tell people. We need to make this huge." Of course, Eric would say the right thing.

"Angie is onto the publicity."

"Who's Angie?" Jack stopped on his way up the stairs.

"You should know. You were the one sucking face with her the first time I met you. Most guys would find out a girl's name first."

"You didn't seem to mind."

"I didn't get much choice in the matter." I hit him with the full force of my bitchface.

"Hey, hey. Stop being angry. Dinner is almost ready. If you are angry, you can't enjoy the food properly. Jack, you should be nicer to Hannah when she comes here to tell you good news."

Jack scowled but didn't say anything. I think he was a little scared of Eric-Mama.

"Are you staying for dinner?" she asked me.

"Yes, stay," said Eric. "Mum always makes way too much food."

"Not that you complain." She laughed and ruffled Eric's hair.

He flattened his hair down but looked at his mum with affection. They had a special kind of warmth between them. Even though I'd been close to Dad, it wasn't all caring and loving like that. It made me feel messed up inside, happy but jealous at the same time. I caught a glimpse of Jack's face. From the look in his eyes, he felt the same way I did.

So much food covered the table – dishes of delicious-looking nibbly things. Before I got poor, I'd never been hungry or even that interested in food. Now it seemed like I had no manners at all and scoffed down every meal I could get.

"This looks awesome. You are so lucky, Eric, to have a mum who's such a good cook."

"What about your mother, Hannah? Doesn't she cook?"

I shook my head. "I don't have a mother. Well, not that I remember. She died when I was really young."

"Ah, you must eat more, then." Eric-Mama took a platter of barbecued meat and piled it onto my plate. I didn't really follow her logic but I wasn't about to complain. "And kimchi. You must eat lots of kimchi. It's the best thing to make you happy."

She handed me a dish of red stuff. It didn't look like it would make me happy. I took some and tasted it. It was strong but not undelicious. I had some more.

"And rice. You have a lovely figure. It's okay if you eat lots."

I laughed. Again, I didn't follow her logic but it seemed funny to eat just because I had a lovely figure.

Eric-Mama fussed around, making sure we ate enough. Eric seemed to get annoyed with her but I loved it. I just worried she fussed too much and didn't eat anything.

"You have to sit down and eat too. After all, you cooked all this delicious food."

But she shook her head. "I can eat any time. I just like seeing you young people eat. Otherwise you just eat junk like McDonald's and get fat."

We all laughed.

"I don't eat McDonald's," said Jack. "It makes me fart."

He grinned at Eric-Mama. His face lit up when he smiled like that and he lost that hard look he normally had in his eyes. It was the first time I'd seen him smile. His entire face changed and the coldness went out of his eyes for a moment. Then he looked at me and the smile disappeared.

"Jackie, we don't talk about those kinds of things at the dinner table."

That just made him grin more, like he'd only said it to get Eric-Mama to chastise him. I could kind of see why. It was nice to have someone caring about what you said.

Then Eric-Mama went into a long story about how she'd made Jack help her make radish kimchi one year and even though he had big muscles, he soon got tired rubbing in all the spices.

"I'm not as strong as you are. You have over fifty years' experience of making kimchi."

"Hey, you cheeky kid. Do I look over fifty? I look barely old enough to have a son Eric's age. He should call me sister, not mama." Then she laughed a huge belly laugh until we all joined in.

"You have great skin," I told her.

She beamed at me.

"I use special Korean beauty masks. All the famous Korean celebrities use them. They are sheets like this." She put a tissue over her face to show me. "Sometimes Jackie and Eric use them too."

I looked at them, expecting them to deny it, but they just looked sheepish.

"So, Hannah. What's a nice girl like you doing managing a band?"

I choked on my kimchi and tried to think of an answer.

"I was studying but figured it'd be better to get some real-life experience. There's only so much you can learn at university, you know? Doing actual work gives you more business experience."

"Ah, but having an education is important too." Eric-Mama glared at Eric after saying this and he kept his head down, eating. I figured that was a sore point between them.

"I'll probably go back and finish sometime."

By the time we'd finished dinner, I didn't think my belly had ever been so full. All that yummy meat and hotpot and so many different things I felt like my mouth was going to explode with the awesomeness of the flavours. I wanted to adopt Eric-Mama and have her cook for me every night.

"Why don't you boys make such happy faces like Hannah?"

Eric laughed. "You really do look happy."

"I love this food. It's the best."

I'd never had a meal where people moaned and groaned over the food and I'd never done it myself but it felt good to express my happiness at eating out loud like that instead of being polite. I'd never sat and patted my belly as it felt tight as a drum after dinner either. Even Eric had loosened the belt on his jeans.

"I'll put some in containers for you to take home with you, if you like."

I wanted to kiss her. I really did want to take some home.

"There's a last bit of pork belly. Do you want it?"

Eric pushed the plate toward me.

"No, I'll explode. Seriously. Well, okaythen."

"I've never seen a woman eat like you," said Eric, and even Jack's mouth turned up at the corners.

Eric-Mama disappeared into the kitchen and returned with a whole bag full of food. More than I'd ever be able to fit in my little fridge but I didn't think it'd last long anyway.

"You remember how to get to the train station?" Eric asked.

"No. Hannah can't go home on the train. Jack, you drive her."

Jack shrugged. Obviously he could not think of anything worse than driving me home.

"I'll be fine. It doesn't take long."

Eric-Mama shook her head. "It's dangerous for such a pretty girl to be alone at the train station at this time of night. There are a lot of bad people around here and you can't run away because your belly is so full. It won't take Jack very long."

"It'll be an inconvenience for him and I didn't even realise he had a car."

"He has a car. Where do you live?"

I told her.

"See, it will take hours for her to get home by train. And it's cold and dark. You don't want her getting attacked by creeps."

Jack picked up his car keys. "Come on."

I shook my head, but Eric-Mama pushed me out the door.

I followed Jack to the garage behind their place.

"This is your car? It's really old."

Jack cocked his eyebrow at me but didn't reply. I guess that came out wrong. I didn't mean old and crappy, but old and wow. I knew nothing about cars, but this car must be worth a mint – and cost a mint to drive. The thing was huge and in immaculate condition. The body shone with a red gloss and it had huge fins out the back. It had to be from the '60s or something. When I opened the door, the smell of old leather really hit me. I wondered if Jack had restored it himself.

The drive home didn't take long but we sat in awkward silence. I tried to think of something to say but my mind was a raging pit of blankness. I didn't want to mention the band in case he got snappy again and I couldn't think of anything else we had in common. I wanted to get home and sleep off my food baby but, at the same time, the thought of his thigh so close to mine sent a buzz through my body. These old cars with their bench seats seemed to invite some kind of sin.

He turned on the stereo.

"Do you know this song?" he asked.

"Screw you, dude," I sneered back. "Do you think I'm a moron?"

I might not have known much about music but this was Elvis. Is there a person alive who doesn't know Elvis?

I curled in my seat and rested my head against the leather. Suddenly, I was eight years old and driving in the car with Dad and "Heartbreak Hotel" had come on the radio and we'd sung together. I don't know where we'd been driving to but I'd completely forgotten that time until now, the soft breeze coming in through the car window and the sun making everything outside shine so bright.

"It's the next left," I said, coming back to the present and realising I was nearly home.

He pulled over outside.

"You live here?"

"Yeah, I live here. It's cool. And very convenient."

He raised his eyebrow. "Really? And I'm not buying that story about dropping out to get 'real world' experience for a minute. Rich chicks like you don't just drop out of school and move into slummy apartments. Not unless they are playing at being *real* people."

"I am a real person. Oh, and thanks for the lift home."

I opened the car door and climbed out.

"Umm, Hannah?"

I noticed he called me by name instead of "babes." I don't know why that made me grin. I ducked my head because I didn't want him to know that made me happy. Instead of answering, he stared at his hands resting on the steering wheel. I couldn't read the expression on his face and waited for some snarky remark.

"Thanks. For organising the gig."

He reached across and shut the door and drove off quickly, leaving me to wonder why I couldn't stop grinning and why my heart was being so stupid.

Chapter 11

So I turned up at the filming location with a heap of clothes I'd begged and borrowed from some very funky designers. All I'd had to say was that we were filming a clip and people happily loaned me stuff. I'd not realised it would be so easy.

The warehouse buzzed with activity. I'd been expecting a couple of Angie's friends with some borrowed cameras – real low-grade stuff – but this was like walking onto a Hollywood set. I almost swooned looking around the place. Then I nearly got knocked down by a guy carrying a bunch of equipment.

"Sorry, sorry," he called as he rushed off.

"Where do I—"

He disappeared before I could ask him where to leave the clothes. I'd slung the bags over my shoulder and they were weighing me down. I couldn't see anywhere to set them up, although Angie had told me she'd have an area organised for wardrobe.

There seemed to be about twenty or more people buzzing around. Across the room, a couple of girls set up a bunch of backdrops, while some guys played around with a big metal box of technical-looking equipment. A couple of other guys laid tracks down on the floor.

In the middle of the filming area stood a huge prop that looked like an old pirate ship with cannons and skull and crossbones flags and rope ladders. It even had a network of sails that looked all piratey and authentic.

"Hey you, get up here and help me fix these gels!"

I looked up and saw a dude hanging off some scaffolding. And he wanted me to help him with his gels? Why did he need his nails done? That just seemed blatantly stupid. Maybe he was messing with me. I figured it was best to ignore him.

"Hey, I asked you to help me. Get your arse up here."

I looked around the warehouse to see who he was actually talking to but there was nobody else nearby.

"Yeah, you. What? Are you stupid or something?"

This guy obviously had a death wish. Could he not see that I wore an outfit not made for clambering? High heels and a skintight pencil skirt pretty much ruled out climbing up scaffolding.

"God, what are you waiting for? Make yourself useful."

"Oi, Peter. Stop giving orders to Hannah. She's the band manager, not your lackey. Hannah, you have the wardrobe? Awesome sauce. Is it all awesome and pirate? The guys are going to look freaken cool in this clip if it kills me. But what if they get super huge and I can't even get tickets to see them play? That'd suck. You'll get me tickets, won't you Hannah? Promise me, no matter what, you'll get me tickets."

She led me over to some racks in the corner so we could hang the clothes.

"Oh, Jack has to wear this frock coat. Imagine how his broad shoulders will look in it. And he has to wear the ruffly shirt with it with that lace. With his leather pants. Oh my god, I'm getting wet just thinking about it."

"Angie!"

"Well, it's true. Don't tell me you aren't?"

"I've told you before—"

"Yeah, yeah. You can say it all you want but I can't believe any woman would NOT be interested in Jack Colt." She grabbed my wrist and held it between her thumb and finger. "You have a pulse, ergo you must be interested. That's just science."

I shrugged. There was no talking sense to her. But I loved her enthusiasm for the costumes. Before this filming had finished, that band would be only too happy to see the back of me as manager.

"That one would be perfect on Eric. Emphasis his cute shyness."

I nodded. I'd picked out the drawstring shirt with Eric in mind.

"And Spud can wear anything, there's no hope for him anyway. We can just put him in the back with dim lighting. The band isn't here yet and I've been running around gangbusters all morning. Come out and have a fag with me until we start."

"I hope they turn up. I have zero faith in Jack Colt."

"You have an agreement with him, right? We worked our arses off getting him that gig." She waved to a guy on the scaffolding as we walked through the warehouse. "They should appreciate what we did for them. They should buy us dinner at a romantic restaurant and flowers and all that kind of thing and Jack Colt should get down on his knees and thank us."

"Not really. It was Frank."

"Yeah, but those bloody kids rolled our tree frog outfits when we took off after jerk face and that was a whole shit fight."

We'd completely forgotten about the bag with our costumes and the posters until later and, when we'd gone back to get them, they'd been stolen. Angie and I had searched the streets but nothing had turned up.

"I'd have made sure they were stolen long ago if I'd thought of it."

She laughed.

We stepped out onto the street and she huddled in a doorway to light her cigarette.

"You are looking smoking hot today. Any particular reason? Huh? Huh?" She nudged me and grinned.

I thought so too but hadn't wanted to say it. Angie wore a pair of short shorts with striped tights and she'd added blue to the green in her hair. She looked pretty hot herself. In a grungy kind of way.

"No reason at all."

Angie thought too much about flirting with the band and not enough about making money from them but still, I didn't know what I'd do without her.

We went back inside and the guys had arrived. Jack Colt stood to one side while three of the girls talked to him and flicked their hair. For a moment, my stomach clenched tight. Bimbos.

Angie clapped her hands loudly, getting their attention.

"Back to work, girls. No time for standing around chatting. You guys, get to make-up."

"Make-up? No way." Jack glared at us.

"It's part of the process. You need to look good on film and those lights will show up every imperfection."

"I don't think he has any imperfections," one of the girls said.

Angie shot her a look to silence her.

"It's not optional," she said and pushed them towards the make-up area.

I didn't really have much to do, so I found a spot out of the way and settled down to watch.

A little while later, Jack Colt returned. I don't know what that make-up artist had done but he looked hot. Super hot. As he walked toward me, my legs turned to jelly. That was stupid. He was still the same person but I'd never noticed how sculptured his cheekbones were, and the dazzling intensity of his eyes was even brighter with all that eyeliner.

I called him over so we could get started on the costumes.

"You want me to wear what?"

I'd held up the velvet coat jacket. It was the perfect blend of pirate and on-trend. The designer had been an absolute doll and I thought the clothes were perfect for the look we wanted.

"I'm the manager. You wear it."

"I said I'd do the video, I didn't say I'd dress up like an idiot." Those eyes flashed at me and for an instant, I wanted to back down and agree to anything he said, just so I could get to see his smile again.

Then I realised that would be letting him win. Why couldn't he do as I asked without it becoming a thing? Maybe I needed to push him more, make him realise that life would be hell with me in charge.

"It's part of the image."

"I have no image."

"You didn't. You do now."

I held out the jacket, waiting for him to take it. Instead he walked away.

Screw that. I was sick of him and the way he walked away or brushed off everything I said.

I ran after him and blocked his way, crossing my arms and staring him down.

"Is this how you treat everything you don't agree with in life? Walking off and not even discussing it? Maybe that's a big part of your problem."

He tried to brush me aside.

"No. Let's talk about this. What do you want? Tell me, instead of just ignoring everything I say."

"I didn't think you cared about what I want. You turn up and tell us you're in charge now. In charge of our band. Now you want us to have an image. What makes you think we want any of this?"

"Well, what do you want? You don't talk to me. You ignore me when I try to discuss the band, so how do I take your wishes into account when I have no bloody idea what they are?"

I stood with my hands on my hips waiting for him to respond. But he said nothing; he just stared at me like I was some kind of freak. I trembled a little inside but I had no intention of letting him see that.

"Look, Jack, it's a video clip. You just need to act out a part. We've got this whole team of people here waiting for you to get to work. You don't want to waste their time, do you? They are all here working for free so that we can get this done and you are acting like some spoilt little prima donna. And you say I'm a princess!"

He didn't answer but he strode back into the warehouse and grabbed the clothes off the rack. I pointed to the change room Angie had rigged up with a sheet but he ignored me and pulled his t-shirt off.

The room went quiet as every head turned toward him. I had figured he had a good body, he didn't try to disguise it with those tight t-shirts he wore, but seeing him half-naked was something else altogether. The muscles down his back rippled as he raised his arms to put the shirt on and the light reflected off his skin, giving it a magical sheen.

I couldn't look away, even though I wanted to ignore what his naked back did to my insides. All the air had been sucked out of the room and everything disappeared except those hard muscles. My fingers twitched to reach out and touch him, to trace the line of his hard shoulders down to that delicious curve of his arm and around his shoulder blade. I wanted to flick my tongue into that tasty indentation.

Then he unzipped his jeans.

I willed myself to look away, to remember what a jerk he'd been, but his thumbs had hooked around the belt loops and he slowly lowered his jeans, exposing the white fabric of his jocks beneath.

He bent over slightly and my vision was filled with that perfect curve of butt. The hollow where the curve started, that space, it belonged to a woman's hands. Holding him as he rose above her in that moment just before he thrust inside.

"Hannah, close your mouth. You're drooling." Angie slapped me on the arm. "I know exactly what you are thinking."

I shook myself, about to deny it, but I could feel the flush in my face and the heat rising through my body. I didn't want to meet her eyes because I knew she'd see something primal there. A part of me I didn't even know existed.

"Let's get started, then." Angie tried to sound all business but she turned to me and motioned fanning herself.

Jack Colt, now fully dressed, strutted over to the set in a way that showed he'd been fully aware of every person watching him. Angie cued up the music for them to lip-sync to and the filming started.

I tried to clear my mind but the images blurred together. Those powerful muscles with the sound of his voice *that* night and the feel of his lips on mine.

"Cut," Angie called. "Spud, can't you even lip-sync to your own song?"

"What? I'm supposed to be lip-syncing?"

Angie had put him in a black-and-white striped t-shirt with a scarf around his head and an eye patch. It kind of worked.

"You are out of time. Can you just maybe hoist the mainsail or something?"

"How do I do that? What's the mainsail?"

"Buggered if I know, but look like you are doing sailor-type things, okay?"

"Okay."

He shrugged and looked confused, shooting a look at Jack. Jack nodded slightly as if to say it was okay. Spud was so his bitch.

"Let's go from the top."

Angie cued up the music again. The song we'd decided to go with, "In Your Pretty Party Dress," was one of my favourites on the CD Eric had given me. I'd kept singing the chorus all the time. That's what you want in a song. Something catchy.

"Cut."

"Again. I'm trying to look sailory."

"Not you this time, Spud. Jack, can you try to look a bit more... well, sexy?"

Angie actually said that? The same Angie who spent half her life talking about how sexy Jack was? The same Angie who'd just been drooling over his butt?

He winked at her.

"I can't look sexy on cue, babe."

Angie pouted. "Sure you can, babe. Just think sexy thoughts. Think of banging some hot chick. Think about it real hard."

She winked right back at him.

Jack turned his gaze to me. A few of the girls turned around, trying to work out who he looked at. Was he thinking of banging me? He could stop that right now. I'd not given him permission to bang me in his head. That made it non-consensual head sex. That had to be wrong. It was bad enough that I'd had to non-consensually hear him get a blow job.

Heat rose through my body. I couldn't meet his eyes but stared at my shoes. I couldn't resist looking back up again, though, to check if he still looked at me. Suddenly, I didn't know what to do with my hands. I tried to move away out of his sight but he'd turned his attention back to the set anyway.

"Want me to help?" asked the make-up chick.

"No, I think Jack can manage it on his own." Angie shooed the girl away with her hands. "Actually, while we are stopped, can you fix Spud's make-up? He seems to be sweating quite a bit."

Jack walked over to Spud and whispered something. The two of them laughed and glimpsed my way. I don't know what they were saying and Jack didn't look at me again after that, but Spud stole a few glances, then laughed.

I ignored them. They could act like little kids if they liked, at least they were doing what I wanted. I managed to get myself hidden away in a corner near the lighting rig. I figured it best just to stay out of the way and I didn't want him looking at me like that. I got out my phone to keep myself occupied while they were filming but he seemed to be at the centre of my vision no matter what I did. I didn't want Jack getting annoyed and storming out again. I wanted to see this filming finished. We'd managed to get use of the warehouse for the afternoon but we had to be out by five o'clock. There was no temper tantrum time built into the work schedule.

Those damn dragons in my game had eaten me because of the bloody distractions, and I decided I'd play again, this time focusing on the game, but looked up a few seconds later to see Jack walking towards me. He had his mouth set in a determined line, like he had something he needed to discuss. It'd be to complain about the clothes, or maybe he'd decided he didn't like the song or something like that. I figured I should just inch out of his line of sight and maybe he'd forget about me.

Then, all of a sudden I heard a yell and spun around. At the same time, I went flying through the air to land on the ground with a thud, and with something on top of me.

Then a throbbing pain started in my side where I'd landed and I yelped. I tried to disentangle myself from the heap on top of me and became aware of arms wrapped around me and a strong thigh wedged between my legs. I felt safe for a moment, and then I opened my eyes and saw Jack Colt's face centimetres from mine. What the hell kind of game was this?

I couldn't breathe. All the air had been knocked out of me.

I tried to talk but I couldn't get words out. The world went black and spinning.

He moved off me and I sat up. Beside us, the smashed pieces of one of the lights lay shattered on the ground.

"What happened?"

Jack didn't answer, though. He just walked off, leaving me dazed and aching.

Angie ran over and smoothed my hair.

"The light fell. Jack saved you. He hurled himself on top of you and shoved you out of the way as it was falling. Oh my god, it was so romantic. He saved your life, Hannah. You could've been dead."

Angie's words went in my ears but it took a while for my brain to process them. My head buzzed and I didn't know if anything would make sense again.

"Hey, what did you say? Jack Colt? More like he'd push me into the way of danger."

"Seriously, he saved you. You'd be mush now. And I'm going to kill Peter. He should be making sure he's doing his work right instead of dicking around. I bet he was too busy perving on Jack's arse to do his job properly."

I figured I should at least thank Jack for saving me. Maybe it was just a gut reaction and he'd do it for anyone. I mean, you don't want to see someone being splattered under a huge light, even if you don't like them. It'd be all messy and gross.

"Are you really okay?" Angie asked. "I don't want to sound like a bitch but we really need to get back to filming."

"Yeah, I'm fine. Just a bit dazed. I'll sit here and recover."

"Sweet. If you feel at all wrong, let someone know. We don't want you to end up passing out or anything. And what was it like, when he fell on top of you? Was it all sexy and rawr?"

It had happened so fast, there was no time to feel sexy and rawr. It just hurt. I rubbed my side. No ribs broken or anything. But my leg throbbed in a very different way from the pressure of his thigh against mine.

Peter had climbed the scaffolding and adjusted the lights. "All ready to go," he called down to Angie. Then he looked at me. "Sorry."

Well, he should be sorry. If I'd died, he'd have been sorry. I'd have sued his arse off, from the grave. Maybe I could sue him? That'd get me some ready cash. Only, who was ultimately responsible for these things? That would be the band, right? And who was the manager of the band…? yikes. I'd have to sue myself, and I so couldn't afford that.

The music started again and they got in place for filming. I pulled a bottle of water out of my bag and took a swig, then settled back to watch.

Chapter 12

Finally Angie called out to say it was a wrap.

"When can we see the final product?" asked Eric.

"Not for a while, but I wanted to ask you about doing some work on the graphics for it. Are you free to help out?"

"Of course. Just let me know."

Angie came over to get her stuff. I packed up the clothes and got them ready to return to the stores. When I tried to pick up the bags, though, I yelped in pain. No way could I lug those bags around town. Shit. I couldn't exactly afford a cab either.

"Are you okay?" Jack Colt appeared out of nowhere.

"I'm fine. I'm perfectly fine."

"No, you aren't. You're whimpering."

"I do not whimper. You make me sound like a drowned kitten or something." I tried to pick up the bags again and made a sound that was definitely not a whimper, though it did sound bloody awful.

"Whimper."

"Whimper or not, I have to get these clothes back to the shops or I'm going to be in a mass of trouble. Unless, of course, you want to buy your outfit to keep. You did seem to get very attached to it."

He was not amused.

"I'll drive you."

I remembered that awkward drive home from dinner. Then imagined that to the power of infinity with all the driving across town.

"I think I can manage."

Jack picked up the bags and walked off without even listening to me. I followed him. If he wanted to drive me, then I guess it was going to happen whether I liked it or not.

He threw the bags in the back of the car.

"Where to first?"

I gave him the address of the store and we took off. He turned on the stereo and even relaxed and sang along to the song.

"What's this song?" I asked.

"You don't know it? Wait, you mean you have never heard this song before? Have you ever heard of the Ramones? Don't tell me, you've been living under a rock for your entire life."

I thought he'd get all snarky and not talk to me but instead he told me about when he was twelve years old and he heard the Ramones for the first time. How he'd never really thought about music before then, but it was like – bam! Something changed in his life.

"Just listen to this bit..." He turned the volume up on the stereo. "That's what it's about. That's the money shot."

And so I listened. I really listened and it wasn't bad at all. Then I looked up to see him smile at me.

"Hey, watch the road."

It seemed to take no time to get to the store. He ran the bag of clothes in, while I rested in the car.

"Okay, there are two more places to go. We might get caught in traffic going to this next place, though. Bloody peak hour."

"No problem," he said.

"More music?"

"Why don't you tell me about you? What's the real reason for you taking on the band management and dropping out of uni? You're living in that crummy apartment, too. Are you slumming it like a poor little rich girl or is there something more?"

I stared out the window. Suddenly, I didn't really want to talk. The car did not move in the banked-up traffic, and I watched a boy walk his dog down the street. They stopped every few steps so the dog could sniff something and even they moved faster than we did. The silence in the car got thicker but I didn't want to break it. If I refused to tell him, it'd break this tentative good feeling between us, but I had no desire to talk about those things.

"You don't want to talk about it?"

"It's complicated."

"Ah, complicated."

He inched along as the traffic started moving, then indicated and swung down a side street. Then raced down another street, not even a street really, but a laneway. He turned so fast that I flew across the car.

"Watch it." If a car came towards us on this street, we'd be dead. There was nowhere to pull over, no room for two cars. I grabbed the door handle with both hands and almost pushed my brake pedal foot through the floor as he drove the car faster.

We got to an intersection and he slammed on the brakes, sending me flying, then wove through the traffic to get to another backstreet and took off again.

I'd stopped talking. I'd stopped even thinking about anything except getting out of this car alive. Maybe I'd have been better off getting a taxi. A taxi would be safer.

Ahead, I saw a light about to turn red. At least he'd stop. Except he didn't. He just went faster towards it, making it barely in time. The car became airborne as we went over a bump in the road.

He laughed. "I love that bit."

I tried to smile. We swung through some more streets and he pulled up outside the second place, this time a warehouse.

He ran in and then I gave him the address of the last place.

"Shouldn't take long," he said.

"Yeah, if you drive like a lunatic."

"Hey. We'd still be stuck back there in that traffic jam if I'd not known the shortcut."

"It's better to arrive alive," I said.

He just shrugged and took off again. I regretted saying anything, because he seemed to take it as a challenge. He drove full speed the whole way, pushing it to make the lights and detouring down laneways and backstreets.

He slammed on the brakes outside the shop.

"See, you're alive."

He grabbed the bag of clothes out of the back and I told him I could walk from there.

"No, wait here for me." He ran his hand through his hair and gave me a hopeful grin.

"Okay, I'll wait." I scrunched up my nose, curious to see what he had in mind.

He made the drop-off, then came out and knocked on my window. I wound it down.

"Come on, let's go for a drink."

"Why are you Mr Friendly all of a sudden?"

He grinned at me, in that way that totally disarmed me. How could he go from being so surly to so charming?

"If you're sticking around, we may as well get to know each other."

My common sense told me that I did NOT want him wanting me to stick around, but the fibres of my being tingled. You can't really turn down a drink from a guy who's saved your life without looking pretty damn ungrateful.

I walked with him to a bar so dark and dingy, it took a while for my eyes to adjust after the glare outside. He strode over to the bar and ordered us both beers.

"I'll get it. You know, to say thank you." I didn't want to make eye contact with him, so I watched the woman behind the bar. It wouldn't take much to believe she had a bat hidden away in case of trouble, and it would take nothing at all to imagine her using it.

"I'll get this one, you can get the next round. Let's play pool."

He punched me on the arm as though I were his best buddy. The happy part of me struggled with the part that waited for this all to fall apart.

"You know how to play?"

I shook my head. "No idea. Where would I have learnt to play pool?"

"Just watch me and learn."

He put his money in the slot and the balls plonked down. Then he got the triangle and set them up.

"I'll break."

I nodded and sipped my beer.

He took his shot and potted a big ball, then took another and missed. He thought he was so good.

"Why don't we have a bet on the game?" I asked. "Isn't that what people do? In movies and stuff?"

"It wouldn't be fair to bet with a beginner."

"It's okay. Just something friendly-like, to make it more interesting." I put my head on the side and smiled at him, all innocent and beguiling.

"Okay. If I win, you tell me the truth about why you're managing the band."

I drew my lips into a tight line and looked away from him.

"I guess that's okay, but you have to tell me why such a bad boy rock star lives in that apartment –"

"It's a shithole old warehouse."

"It's worth a bomb. I know real estate and that place can't be cheap. And that car of yours, it's not within the means of a rocker playing dive bars either."

He shrugged and looked away, but his little subterfuge didn't work on me. There was money there somewhere and you couldn't hide it.

"Fine. Loser spills the beans." He drained his beer.

I grabbed the cue, gripping it tightly, and walked around the table, deciding where to shoot from. I finally settled on a spot and leaned over the table, propping the cue on one hand while gripping it in my right.

"Wait, let me show you how to hold it. Otherwise this'll be like taking candy from a baby."

He unpeeled my fingers from the end of the cue and adjusted them, then leaned over me to correct my other hand. The heat of his body rubbed against mine and I could smell that same citrusy scent I'd noticed when I'd woken up in his bed. With his arms around me like that, I could barely think. I was sure the beating of my heart ricocheted right through him. I ordered it to stop. I would not react to his closeness to me. I didn't feel a thing. He could rub against me all he liked; he could leave his hand lingering on mine and his lips just millimetres from my ear. It did nothing whatsoever.

I squirmed away from him.

"I think I can manage on my own," I said, my voice choking.

I hit out, sending the balls flying. My red ball stopped just near the far pocket.

"Oopsies," I said. "I really thought that would go in."

"Better luck next time."

I went to the bar to get more beers while he took his shot.

He'd sunk a couple of balls while I'd gone but had done no real damage.

A few shots later and he'd sunk most of his balls but I had mine covering the pockets.

"Are you sure you haven't played before?" He narrowed his eyes, appraising me.

"Huh? I've not even got one ball in yet. I thought I'd at least have beginner's luck."

I tried to look upset, even stuck my bottom lip out in a pout, but he'd begun to get suspicious. No help for it, then, I might as well finish this game off.

I walked up to the table and potted my balls one after the other. As I lined up the black to finish the game, he stared at me.

"You bitch. You pool-sharking bitch."

The black rolled into the hole, nice and smooth.

"Okay, maybe I have played once or twice before. My dad taught me when I was a kid."

"That's so cheating."

"That's so cheating." I mocked his voice. "Hah, if you wanna play with the big boys, you gotta learn how to take it. And if you are sucker enough to believe all that *I'm just a beginner* bullshit, then you deserve what you get."

"Best of three?" He ran his hand through his hair and looked at me with faint hope in his eyes.

"Best of three is for crybabies."

A couple of greasers walked into the back room. They sized up the two of us and nudged each other. One was tall and thin with rat eyes. He had long hair tied back in a ponytail and wore a long overcoat even though it was quite warm in the bar.

"Up for a game of doubles?" he asked.

The other one was short and fat. He wore a stained t-shirt and had a couple of missing teeth. He leered at me like he could see through my clothes. It made me shudder just to have his eyes on me.

"Yeah, sure," Jack said. "I'm just teaching my missus how to play, though, so we aren't real good."

He was trying that trick on these guys? Couldn't he tell they were pros? Better to just leave now than try it on. The taller one looked like he could even have a knife in his pocket. I tried to shoot Jack a look to warn him but he ignored me.

"I'll get us some drinks."

He grabbed me.

"Do your stuff," he whispered in my ear.

I shook my head. "We don't want to mess with these guys. They look dangerous."

His hand cupped my elbow and I could feel his body leaning in close to me while his breath tickled through my hair. I put my arm around his waist, figuring it was better for the thugs to think we were together than that I was single.

"But I've put a hundred bucks on this game."

He squeezed my arm tighter.

I forced out a laugh. The two thugs glared at us and could quite easily snap. The walls of the room closed in and the air had been sucked out. This situation would not get any better.

"Oh, babes, don't be so dirty," I said and play-slapped him.

I rolled my eyes at the tall thug as though Jack was being a bit naughty, then walked up to take my shot.

I hit the white ball so it skimmed our balls and hit one of theirs, giving them two shots.

Jack raised his eyebrow but didn't say anything. The short, fat thug sidled up to Jack, blowing his stinky breath on him.

"You shoulda taught your woman better."

He held out his hand for the cue. Jack had rolled up the sleeves on his t-shirt to show his tats but they seemed so tame compared to the homemade "love" and "hate" on this guy's hand. They looked like the type of tattoos you'd do while you had time to kill. In jail.

When Jack had his shot, his stupid ego took hold and he sunk two balls. The walls moved in even closer. There was no way we'd be getting out of there alive. Even less chance if we actually won the game. They'd beat us up and then take the money anyway. I'd rather just hand them the money and skip the physical pain.

The tall guy moved over and hovered near me. My hands went all clammy and I was glad it wasn't my shot. He reached over and squeezed my butt. I jumped away but he just laughed.

"I shoulda bet for this one insteada money. You don't wanna throw her into the deal as well, do ya?"

The hairs on the nape of my neck bristled. I reached out for my beer and moved out of his grasp.

Jack shook his head. "She's not on offer, sorry."

As the thug took his shot, Jack gestured to me. I had no idea what his wild hand signals meant. I nodded my head towards the front bar and hoped he'd be ready to flee when I did.

"Your shot, darlin'."

The thug moved towards me like he planned to grope me again. Jack moved towards the doorway. That gave me hope that he'd show some sense. Jack reached over to whisper in my ear.

"I don't have any cash on me."

Fuck.

If I messed up this shot, we'd be in the shit. With no money to pay them, the thugs would skin us alive. If I won the game for us, they'd beat us and probably skin us alive anyway. The only option was to flee.

I leaned across the table, keeping my eyes on the thugs, then aimed straight at the black ball, getting it in the side pocket.

"Our game," said the shorter one. He looked at me, licking his lips.

"Back in a sec, must be my shout," I said. I strode to the bar, like I had every intention of returning. Jack waited in the bar. He saw me, grabbed my hand, and we fled from the bar. I thought he'd run back to his car, but once he started running, he kept going. We ran down the cobblestoned laneway behind the bar, crisscrossing through the connecting streets. He dragged me along by the hand, forgetting I wore heels that got caught between the stones. Every time I stumbled, he jerked me up. The pain shot up my side but I kept running, figuring it was better to put up with it than to let those thugs catch us.

"Are they following us?" I panted when we finally stopped.

"I don't think so. We've got a fair bit of distance behind us and they didn't look very fit."

I bent over, trying to get my breath back. He put his arm around me.

"Are you okay? I forgot about the accident earlier."

"Oh yeah, thanks for that. Saving my life and all that."

"You probably wouldn't have died. You might have just had some brain injury or something. Nothing you'd notice much."

I punched him on the arm.

I steadied myself and leaned against the stone wall. My chest heaved, each deep breath making my breasts rise and fall.

"How are we going to find our way back to the car?"

Now I'd stopped running, all the pain flooded my body. The burning in my calves, the blisters on my heels and the dull ache in my side.

Then I noticed him staring at me.

"What are you looking at?"

"Nothing." But he didn't take his gaze from mine, then he reached over and brushed my hair back from my face.

I gulped, then we both laughed.

Then the laughter disappeared from his eyes, replaced with the same look he'd given me during filming. I couldn't meet that look, figuring it would drown me. It churned my stomach and heated my body.

I giggled nervously as the heat from my body settled between my legs.

He grabbed my wrists and drew my hands over my head. A shudder went through me from the tips of my fingers right down to my feet. I struggled to break free from his grip but he held me so tight I knew it was pointless and I knew the look in my eyes was telling him "yes" even while I tried to break free of him.

He moved in so that the length of his body was against mine. His chest pressed against my breasts, feeling my hard nipples, his legs wrapped around mine, his cock rubbing against me.

Every part of me yearned for him to kiss me, and my struggling now became a writhing to get closer to him, to press him against me and feel his hardness.

Then he kissed me.

He kissed me like I was his for the taking. Not the slow, teasing kiss of that first time, but sure and rough and demanding.

His mouth crushed into mine, his tongue ramming inside me. Flesh on hot flesh. My leg rising up to circle his waist.

While he had my arms pinned against the wall, my hips thrust against him, grinding into him. His mouth moved from my lips to my neck, sucking and biting. I squirmed tighter against him.

This was a bad, bad thing but I didn't want to stop. The adrenalin from running coursed through my body, heightened by his kiss. This was bad, bad, bad. The refrain kept going through my mind, but somehow, the thought of the badness just made me hotter.

He let go of my wrists and moved away from me, but I grabbed his hips, that hollow I'd noticed earlier, and pulled him closer.

At that moment, I wanted him and to hell with the consequences. I wanted him to take me, right there against the wall in that dark alley. I rubbed myself against him, against his hard cock, my fingers entangled in his hair, his fingers stroking my breasts. Heat emanated from our bodies, all sweaty from the run and getting sweatier. His skin tasted salty under my tongue.

I moaned as his fingers worked their way down, to feel the wet cotton of my panties between my legs. I moved against his fingers as they inched their way inside the elastic. I needed to have him, his fingers, his cock, anything.

And then...

"Look, pashers!" I heard a voice call out. Then some kids giggled.

Jack pulled away from me and swung toward them but they'd run off, their foot-thuds and laughter echoing down the alleyway.

I straightened my skirt and ran my fingers through my hair. I knew they were just a couple of kids but it struck me how I must have looked to them. I'm not one of those girls who spread her legs as soon as some guy acts nice towards her and I'd seen for myself how Jack Colt treated women. How he could be so nice to their face, then talk mean about them behind their back. I'd seen how he changed from his hurt, vulnerable little boy act, to nasty and snarling.

If I let him near me, he'd be like a wrecking ball, destroying everything in his wake.

Hannah, I told myself, you have to be stronger than anyone.

But I couldn't meet his eyes and as we walked back to the car, I still ached for his touch.

Well, not so much walked as hobbled. My feet had been torn to shreds on the run. I'd been too pumped to notice, but now every step made me wince.

"Lean on me," Jack said.

I shook my head.

"Don't be stupid, you can't walk."

He put his arm around me and supported my weight. I tried not to limp, but with each step, the pain got worse.

"You should take your shoes off," he said.

"You're kidding. Who knows what's on the ground? Broken glass. Syringes."

"True," he said, then swept me into his arms.

I wanted to protest and make him put me down but it was the only way to get home. I kept my body stiff and resisted the urge to sink into him and lean my head against his chest. I held my breath so his scent didn't disarm me.

"You're a lot heavier than you look," he said.

"I can walk." I struggled to get out of his arms but he gripped me tighter.

"It's okay, I skipped my workout today."

Then we got back to the main street and he put me down for a rest.

"I can walk home from here," I said. My place was only a block away.

He hesitated and looked at me as if he wanted to say something, but held back. Was he expecting me to invite him home?

The silence between us stretched out uncomfortably but I couldn't say those words. The gates had come down, the steel wall erected. And, even if I wanted to invite him home, the thought of my crummy room stopped me. He'd thought it looked bad from the outside; what would he think if he could see the inside? It was one thing for him to believe I was a rich princess who was playing at this, but if he knew the truth, if my image of being that perfect princess shattered, what would happen then?

Chapter 13

"We've got the CDs? Please tell me we have the CDs. I can't remember putting the box in the cab."

"Take a deep breath. I've got them right here." Angie nudged me in reassurance. Kind of like a pat on the arm when your arms are stacked full of boxes.

"Great. I'm sure we've forgotten something. We do have all the boxes?"

"There's still another load outside. That damn cab driver coulda helped us carry them in, lousy bastard. Hopefully no one will steal them."

I put the boxes down and sighed.

"They stole our tree frog costumes from around here, remember. If they'll steal those, they'll steal anything."

We looked at each other, then ran outside to grab the rest of the boxes.

"That's five hundred CDs plus all the t-shirts and posters? Are you sure that's not too much stuff? This is all my money invested in merchandise. If we don't sell anything, I'm ruined. And I'll be wearing Storm t-shirts for the rest of my life."

"Relax. I told you, we have to look like we mean business. We can't have a shit stall with nothing on it. No one's going to touch that shit. And I've talked a few friends into coming along. Plus, check out these t-shirts."

Angie opened one of the boxes and pulled a t-shirt out.

"Sexy t-shirt is totally sexy! Eric is a genius. The design is amayonnaising. You wouldn't even need to be into Storm to want one of these."

She ripped off the t-shirt she wore and stood in just her black lace bra. Did I mention that the foyer had plate glass windows that anyone on the street could look through?

"Angie!"

She slipped the t-shirt over her head.

"It's okay, Hannah. It's not like I'm showing anything, no worse than wearing a bikini at the beach."

That might be true but it seemed indecent. You could see her nipples through that bra.

"And don't stress. If we sell two hundred t-shirts, we break even. Anything over that is pure profit."

"That sounds like a lot of t-shirts to me. Where do we set them up? What do we do here? I have no experience at this kind of thing."

All thought of being a purposely shitty manager and getting out of this contract had emptied out of my head. I could not fail at this. Not something this big and public.

"Ah, there you are." Sleazy Jason came through a side door, his booming voice echoing around the empty room. "You can stack all that in there."

He nodded toward a door, obviously a store cupboard or something. We hauled the boxes over while Jason watched and nodded his head. I'm all for women's equality and that kind of thing, but what was with these guys letting us do all the heavy lifting?

"Okay, what now?"

"Is the band ready to sound-check? They only have a small window of time before the next band needs to use the stage, so if they don't get here soon, they'll miss out."

I had no idea where they were.

"Give Jack a call," said Angie. "It'll screw things up if they don't sound-check."

"I don't want to." Okay, that might have sounded a bit whiny.

Angie gave me a searching look. I wasn't about to tell her anything, though.

Luckily we were interrupted by a knock on the glass. Eric waved at us and I pointed to the unlocked side door.

"You guys set them up," I said. "I need the bathroom."

I really did not want to see Jack Colt even though my pulse raced and all the colours around me seemed more vivid. That was just nerves, not excitement about him being so close.

I didn't want to think about him. About *that*. About Jack Colt and that kiss.

I hadn't been able to get it out of my head, though. I should never let him kiss me. I should never have returned his kiss.

But, when his lips pressed against mine, my brain stopped working and the world contracted into a tiny circle that was just him and me and the sensations of our bodies moving together.

I'd not heard from him since and I couldn't call him. I just couldn't.

When I got out of the bathroom, the sounds of them tuning their gear filled the main room. Angie jumped around, all excited.

"I get to watch them sound-check. This is the coolest thing ever. I never hoped to do anything this cool. I'm going to take some photos to post on the blog. And we get to hang out with them afterwards, right? Ah, my life is so sweet."

I laughed at her.

"Everything ready for tonight?" Sleazeball Jason appeared beside me. "Now, remember, onstage at nine o'clock exactly and off at nine forty-five. The band gets two free drinks each and they have to be out of the back room by ten forty-five. You can set up your stuff for sale out the front just before the doors open. We don't get that good a crowd in on a Tuesday night normally, so if they drag some people in, who knows in future."

After the sound check, we waited for the guys to pack up their gear. The next band waited to hit the stage – three hulking guys and a tiny chick with piercings and tattoos and her hair dyed various shades of pink. She huddled in a big fake-fur coat of neon pink on one of the guitar cases, playing with her phone, oblivious to everything.

Jack Colt kept glancing over at her. She didn't pay him any attention, though, just kept on playing *Candy Crush Saga* or whatever it was she was doing. A lump of big horrible stuff bounced around my stomach as I watched him looking at her. Of course, she was the kind of girl he liked. She looked all alternative and dirty. The kind of girl who would not even hesitate to take him back to her apartment.

The guy that was with them, the older guy who wore a leather jacket but didn't wear it well, and jeans that seemed a little bit too dark and a little bit too short, walked up to Jason and they high-fived each other.

"How you going, bro?" he asked.

They walked off, chatting and laughing. Is that how a manager was supposed to act? I wondered if I should watch him and take notes but, no matter what, I would not stoop to dressing so badly. I'd not stoop to being all buddy-buddy with that sleazeball either. When Storm became hugely famous, I'd never have to deal with shits like him again. I'd be laying down the terms. Learjets, cases of champagne backstage, and money. Lots of lovely money.

Angie nudged me.

"The guys are going to get something to eat, come on."

If my belly had felt upended watching Jack look at that clown girl, it totally took a nosedive now. What would I say to him? How would I react? I didn't want anyone knowing what had happened the other night. It didn't mean anything anyway. It was just a few too many beers and then the adrenalin rush from racing through the streets. I'd look like a fool if I took it to mean anything more than that.

As we walked down the street, Angie and I lagged behind while she jumped around. For her, this was the greatest day ever.

For me, I had too many emotions and too many head things to deal with. But it was good just to enjoy her excitement.

"A burger joint? This is the glamorous rock star life?" Angie asked.

"Sure is," said Eric. "Nothing like a burger before a gig."

We settled into a booth. Jack avoided my eyes. I avoided his. Well, I tried to, when I wasn't checking to see if he was still avoiding mine. I wondered if he hated me or if he had just been playing around the other night and had forgotten all about it. I figured he'd probably be picking up another chick tonight. Probably that singer chick, from the way he'd looked at her.

When the food came out, he picked at it, moving the food around his plate.

"Don't you want that?" asked Spud and grabbed for Jack's burger.

"Nah, you have it."

"Are you nervous?" asked Eric.

I looked at Jack again. He laughed.

"As if. I'm just not hungry."

"You guys are going to rock tonight. It's going to be the greatest gig ever. I've got a few people coming along. Everyone wants to support you."

"How many people?" Eric asked. "I've had nightmares that we'd be playing to an empty room. I mean, who comes out on a Tuesday night? Especially to see the opening band. No one bothers going to see the opening band."

Jack tapped his fingers on the table. As much as he said he wasn't nervous, he couldn't hide it. He seemed full of energy, like a wound-up spring. That was good, I guess. He needed all this energy when he got onstage.

I tried to swallow a bite of my burger but it became a dry, tasteless lump in my mouth.

In the end, Spud wolfed down my burger too.

"You'll be sick, playing drums after eating all that," said Angie.

"No way. I enjoy a good feed."

As we walked back to the venue, I noticed a line of people on the street. Not a huge line, not a going-around-the-block line, but enough people to look like it was more than just milling around on the street. I nudged Eric.

"Doesn't look like you'll be playing to an empty room."

He grinned.

"Are they here to see us?"

"Looks that way," said Angie. "Told you I invited some people."

"You're amazing," said Eric.

Angie's face lit up. She tried to reply but she just stammered. The guys went in the backstage door and I followed them to make sure everything was ready.

"Do you need anything? Drinks? Towels?"

Eric shook his head.

"I guess we'd better set up the merchandise, then," I said to Angie.

We lugged the boxes to the front lobby and set up the rickety card table. Angie grabbed some hangers and climbed on a chair to display the t-shirts and posters.

The other bands turned up with their merchandise.

"We have to make our stuff look the best," Angie whispered to me. "Look at their ugly t-shirts."

I grinned at her. Our stuff did look a lot better.

"That idiot Jason said we couldn't use tape to put up the posters but look at this wall. It's got tape marks all over it. He's so full of shit, just likes throwing his weight around. *I'm Mr Big Important Band Booking Guy. Oh no, you can't use tape on my walls.*"

I tapped her on the leg as I saw Jason walking towards us and we both forced a smile on our faces.

"The doors will open in a couple of minutes."

I nodded. Would anyone even buy this stuff? Before, the band had run down to the local print shop and got a dozen or so shirts printed off before each gig. It'd cost them nearly as much as they sold them for. Pretty much a zero-profit game. Eric had explained it wasn't about the money. If people wore the shirts, it gave the band publicity.

I figured we could make more money if I got a bulk lot of shirts printed. Not only cheaper, but heaps better quality too. Eric had almost squealed when he'd seen his design on them.

"Hannah, you have to put on a t-shirt. We can't sell them if you aren't wearing one."

"I'm not stripping off like you. Not with all those people outside, especially."

I slipped an oversized t-shirt over my outfit, figuring I just needed to wear it while I sat there.

Then the doors opened and people flooded inside. Excitement buzzed in the air and soon we had our first customers. Two girls wearing the old t-shirts.

"Hey, Angie."

"You made it," she said, jumping up to give them a hug. "You have to get the new shirts. They are so much better than the old ones."

She nodded and turned to the next lot of customers. They all seemed to know her by name.

Soon, we had a line at the table. I'd organised a system of sizing with the boxes but we ended up in chaos, trying to get everyone through as quickly as possible.

"Do you know all these people?" I asked her. It seemed like everyone greeted her and stopped by to say hello.

"How many people do you think are here? Do you think we'll get five thousand?"

Angie shrugged.

"I dunno, but we've sold enough t-shirts to get your money back."

I quickly hugged her, even though I'm not a hugger, and got back to serving.

People still kept coming in.

"Hey, Angie. Great to get out and support the band. Thanks for letting us know about tonight."

"No problem."

"Do you have a large?"

"Sorry, we've sold out. Try an XL."

Had I heard right? We'd sold out of larges? I tried to work out quickly in my head how many we'd ordered and the profit margin on that many t-shirts, but the maths made my head spin.

Inside the main doors, we could hear people chanting for the band to come onstage. *Storm, Storm, Storm.*

The line began to dwindle and those left thrust their money at us in a rush to get inside.

Then the crowd went quiet. A tense silence filled the place, as if every single person was sucking in their breath and it affected the oxygen levels.

"If you want to go in and watch, I'm fine here on my own."

"Are you sure? Are you sure it'll be okay?"

"Of course. Look at how much work you've done getting people here. We'd be nothing without you. The least I can do is let you go in and watch the band. Get going..."

With that she ran off.

I sat at the table, pretty much alone except for some stragglers coming in the door.

People screamed and I imagined the band walking onstage. Then the sound of guitar cut through the screams and it all went mad.

Jack's voice rang out from the stage, full of energy and charisma. I knew this song now. I sang along quietly as he got to the chorus and could hear the crowd singing along too and yelling at the appropriate places. They loved it; they loved him.

The crowd went crazy after the song finished. The screaming and yelling continued into the next song. This was a new one, one I'd never before. It started slow and sexy, like the melody crept up on you, sliding around your body. I couldn't make out the words, just the feeling of intimate longing, building up.

Then they crashed into the crescendo. Energy exploded from inside like a force of nature, a crazy energy that made the hair on the back of my neck stand up.

I grabbed the cash box and raced through the door. Even at the back, the crowd squeezed tight together. I couldn't believe there were so many people. I'd seen them come in, in dribs and drabs, but actually having the mass of them in one room, lit by the multicoloured lights and moving as one, made them look magical.

All eyes were turned to the stage, and centre of that stage stood Jack Colt. He seemed to be in a world of his own, untouchable and aloof. He strutted around, caressing the microphone as though seducing a woman, the same way he'd touched me. A shudder went through every woman in the crowd, all of them thinking the same thing. He whispered the lyrics into the microphone in a voice that sent shivers down my spine.

Then, as the tension grew tangible, they thundered into sound. A wall of sound and wailing. Without even realising, my hips moved in time with the music. My foot tapped. This was awesome. Beyond awesome.

Angie rocked up beside me.

"He's on fire tonight."

I nodded.

He moved over to Eric and the two of them leaned up against each other as they played. The bond between them was so strong. I'd not even realised until I saw them onstage like this. They moved together as one, back to back. Then Jack broke away and ran back to centre stage in time for the chorus.

The crowd became an amorphous mass, the energy intensifying as the music reached its climax. They'd blended together, all their energy and all their dreams merged into one and concentrated on that man with the guitar.

He seemed to sparkle up there. All his indolence and arrogance disappeared, to be replaced by someone honest and true. Someone who spoke to people straight to their hearts. And it didn't hurt that he looked like a god. A woman would have to be blind, deaf and dumb not to react to those hips, swerving and grinding as though he wanted to have hot and dirty sex just with you. Yet, at the same time, he made you feel that he was vulnerable and needed protecting. And that was a lethal combination.

I could hear girls screaming "Jack Colt, Jack Colt" until it sounded like an echo of "Jacolt, Jacolt."

At the end of their set, the crowd screamed for more, going absolutely fanatical. It seemed amazing to me but I had no idea about this kind of thing. Maybe crowds always made the kind of noise that would lift the roof off a place.

Jason appeared beside me. "Get them back out there. They have to do an encore."

"But it's after nine forty-five..."

"Don't care, the second band can go on late."

I thrust the cash box at Angie and pushed my way through the crowd, flashing my pass at the bouncers.

"What the hell are we going to play? We planned a forty-five-minute set. We didn't practice anything else."

Jack paced the small back room, emotions playing out on his face.

"Stop bitching, Jack, and just get out there." I gave him a shove. This was his moment. The crowd were lapping it up and he had to give them more. This was proof, proof that they could make it. "Play one of the same songs again. Play '*Party Dress.*'"

As they headed back onstage, the crowd went insane. I thought a couple of those girls would implode.

The second band sat backstage, waiting for their turn to play.

"We might as well pack up and go home," said one of them. "We can't play after that."

"Tell me about it. This is going to be one of those gigs that people talk about for years to come. Everybody is going to say they were here. It's going to be one of those pivotal moments in rock gigs. And we have to play after that!"

"Speak for yourselves," said the chick, looking up from her phone. She'd changed into a corset and a skintight skirt with long black gloves and crimson lipstick. "I want to stick around and find out more about this Jack Colt."

Even that didn't bring me down from my high. I floated out of the room. This was it. I'd get them signed, I'd get them famous. And I'd solve all my financial problems. *Learjet and champagne, here I come. Designer wardrobe, I'll replace you all.*

No way would I lose that contract. No way would I sell the company. I had to stick around and see what my band could do.

I pushed my way back through the crowd, most of them going crazy. The stage was dark. In a moment, the craziness would explode and I'd have no chance of getting back to Angie unharmed. And then it started and I got knocked around like a pinball in a machine.

"This one's for Hannah," Jack screamed from the stage and I thought I would die right there.

As I got to the back of the room, I saw Frank. He'd turned up. I waved but he didn't see me. As I approached, I noticed the man standing beside him. I stopped dead, and even the roar of the crowd faded in my ears.

Dad.

Chapter 14

My dad had been crazy rich. It'd always been the two of us against the world and nothing was too good for me. We had the big house with maids, plus a beach house that was more luxurious than most people's everyday houses. I'd gone to the best schools and I'd worn the best clothes. Even though I had friends, most of the time I ignored them and went straight from school to Dad's office. I'd sit on a chair beside him and play business, then he'd put me on his shoulders and take me around to meet the staff.

"One day, this will all be yours, honey." That's what he'd say to me.

I'd laugh. It seemed silly to me as a kid because I thought it was all mine anyway. All the offices. All the buildings he'd take me to see that were his. All the meetings where I played on the floor while he talked business.

When I got older, I'd still go to the office. Sometimes I'd go with him to meetings. But sometimes he'd tell me to run home.

"It's no place for a young girl," he'd say.

I'd pout but he'd never change his mind.

I'd expected this to go on forever. I'd get my degree, then work with him in the business. I'd never have to worry about finding a job because all this would be mine one day.

I had it planned out. While I'd had a few boyfriends in high school, when I met Tom the plan had fallen into place. He came from a similar family and everyone said it would be the perfect relationship. Our businesses would merge when we married and we'd run them together. I never thought about things like excitement or fun in a relationship because that would come from the business.

We'd gone away to university together. Tom wanted to get into the best law program in the country and I followed behind him, thinking moving to another state would be an adventure. Although, to be honest, my life didn't really change that much. Same life, different place.

Then, a few months ago, Frank called me and told me to pack my things and come home.

"Is Dad ill?" I asked.

"No, nothing like that. I can't really explain over the phone."

I'd packed up my bags and headed home, feeling a bit exasperated. It wasn't long until exams and I needed to study. I didn't really have time for family drama.

When I got off the plane, Frank was waiting for me.

"Where's Dad?" I asked. I had a horrible feeling Frank had been lying about him not being ill. Otherwise, why wasn't he there to pick me up himself? Why hadn't he phoned himself? None of this made sense.

"He's... well, we aren't sure where he is at the moment."

He didn't say much else until we got back to his house. I had a feeling he didn't want to tell me in front of the driver, so I didn't push it. I spent that ride from the airport with my face against the window of the car, trying not to think of all the possibilities.

Then finally he got the chance to explain.

"I'm not sure how it happened. Your dad, he got into some trouble. Got in over his head. I tried to warn him, but he was always a gambler. He thought the risks would pay off in the end. And maybe, if he'd had more time, it would've worked out..."

I didn't really understand what he was trying to say.

"Dad had some business troubles?"

"The worst kind. He's lost, well, pretty much everything."

I sunk down on the sofa, not comprehending. Dad had lost money. He'd done that before. He said you couldn't make an omelette without breaking some eggs. But he always bounced back.

"But it's no big deal, right? He can just move some money from somewhere else to cover it?"

"There is no 'somewhere else' this time, I'm afraid. He's moved it all. It's all gone. Things have been going bad for a while. And, this is really hard..." Frank got up to pour himself a drink. He poured me one too and set it down in front of me. "I'm sorry to tell you this, honey, but some of the stuff your dad was involved in... it wasn't all aboveboard."

I shook my head. No way would Dad be involved in anything dodgy.

"All the company's assets have been frozen. The houses, the cars, everything. There is talk of—"

"Shut up! Just shut up. You're making this up."

I stood up. It couldn't be true. I covered my ears, not wanting to hear any more.

Frank put his arm around me, but I threw him off. Everything went black. I picked up the glass of whiskey he'd poured for me and threw it at the wall.

"Where's he gone? Where's Dad? I need to hear this from him. He'll tell the truth. He'll look after me. He always has."

"He's disappeared. I don't know where he is. I don't know when he'll be back. He called me last night and then the police arrived. I had to try to sort things out. I've got your clothes. They took everything else. All your jewellery, the furniture, all your things. I said your clothes were personal effects. The rest is gone."

I shut my eyes.

"But I still have my allowance, right?"

Frank shook his head.

"But I can go back to uni. I have my flat and—"

Frank shook his head again.

"That was under the company name. I'm organising to get everything shipped down here. Until this is sorted out, it's best you don't go back there."

I could not think about this. I could not even imagine having nothing. People couldn't just take all your stuff. We'd find some money and I'd go back to uni and everything would be okay. Dad would sort it out.

"I'd offer to let you stay here for a while, but even that might not be a good idea. There are people, not just the police, looking for your dad. You should stay under the radar for a while."

"Am I in danger?" This was a nightmare. I'd wake, surely, and find out it was all lies.

"No, but you don't want to be in the spotlight right now. We're trying to keep it out of the papers, but once people find out, this is going to explode, and you don't want to be hounded by them."

I'd packed up my stuff and left with a quick goodbye to Frank. I know it wasn't his fault, but I didn't want to be around him. It made me feel sick.

I'd booked into a hotel. Stupid move, I know now, but at the time I thought it'd blow over in a couple of days. I had money in my bank account. I had my credit cards. Well, I thought I had my credit cards until I tried to use them. Do you know how humiliating it is to have your credit card rejected?

I didn't do much after I checked into the hotel. I didn't want to contact anyone I knew and I couldn't go shopping. I'd go to the pool and swim lap after lap, hoping it would resolve something. After that, I'd fall into bed, exhausted. When I wasn't swimming, I studied, expecting to still get back to school in time for exams.

A few days later, Frank called me to see how I was getting on. He had my stuff sent to the hotel and called in to take me to lunch. That's when he'd told me about the management company. Dad had put the company in my name for some reason. I had no idea why he couldn't have done that with one of the houses, at least, or something of value.

"All this will be yours one day," he'd said, but now "all this" had gone. Disappeared in a way that made my head spin.

"What am I supposed to do with a band management company? I didn't even know Dad had such a thing."

"It was a bit of a hobby for him. Back in the day, when some of his mates played in bands, it was actually his first business. Before all the property development and all that. Then there was that time..."

Frank didn't finish what he was saying. I ignored it until later.

We had some more wine and Frank looked around the hotel.

"I hate to say this, but you really should think of moving out of here. You know when the money's gone, there'll be no more. Maybe you can get some kind of support from the government until you get a job."

I just stared at my wine glass. I couldn't eat any more. The thought of food made me sick. I had no idea about getting a job or anything else. All I knew was how to spend money. And where could I move to?

When I got back to my room, I checked my bank balance and worked out how many days I could stay at the hotel. The answer was not many. I went online and looked at apartments.

I had just over two thousand dollars in my account. That was it. That was all the money in the world. When I looked at apartments, I realised I'd need money for a security bond and a month's rent. Even with the most optimistic calculations, that seemed impossible.

I got the paper and looked for cheaper places, and then happened to see an ad for a place – no bond, no references needed. Pay by the week.

That's how I ended up with my rathole apartment. I figured I could put up with it for a few days. But the days stretched to weeks.

The first night I moved in, I couldn't sleep at all. Every noise in the night was someone ready to cut my throat and steal the things I had left. I moved my dresser in front of the door in case the latch didn't hold and I kept a hammer next to my bed. The wind rattled the old wooden windows in their frames all night and kept me jumpy. My pulse rate did not settle until dawn, when I fell into an exhausted sleep.

When I finally woke up, I made my way to the bathroom but looked at the mouldy shower. I couldn't shower in that. I just couldn't. I'd be dirtier than when I started. As I went back to my room, the old lady from the room down the hall grabbed my hand and told me all about her health condition. I didn't want to know. And she smelt like she'd already died, anyway. I ran away, back to my room, and cried for the rest of the day.

You can only cry for so long, though. I had five hundred dollars left by then, after paying rent and buying food. I got out the papers Frank had left with me and then looked up the details of the band on the Internet. They were playing that Friday night at a bar across town.

I'd asked Frank if I could sell the management company. He'd said it was possible but I should hold on to it. It was the only asset I had now.

"But I just need money until Dad gets back, right?"

Frank had sighed and rolled his eyes but agreed to help me.

I'd put on my most severe outfit, the one that said power bitch, and got on the bus to go to the bar. That's how it had all started.

Chapter 15

Now, you'd think I'd have been totally over the moon to see Dad again. He could fix this mess. He would look after things and say it was all going back to the way it had been. But, when I saw him, my stomach lurched. Instead of running to him, my feet stayed cemented to the ground. My old life had been perfect, so why didn't I want it back?

I watched as all the shouts and cries flooded the room with noise, then I turned and went to find Angie.

"What's wrong?" she asked, but I didn't want to go into it.

"Nothing. Let's get this shit organised so we can get everyone as they come out. I'm wishing now that we'd invested in more stock. At least we won't have to lug those heavy boxes home, right? That's a good thing."

Angie gave me a quizzical look, but then she grinned, not willing to push it any further.

Then the band finished. It'd be fairly quiet until after the headline act, Angie had said, but people flooded out the doors before the next band even started.

"What do you mean you have no t-shirts left?" a girl asked me. "Can I go on the mailing list so I can get one?"

I looked at her in confusion but Angie whipped out some paper and a pen.

"Put your details on there and we'll get you sorted."

Inside, the sound of the next band started but the energy had gone from the room. I almost felt sorry for them, playing to a few of their friends.

The line got longer and longer. I swear half these people had already bought stuff before. Then, to make it worse, Eric came out and decided to help us, but that just meant more people flooded around us so he could sign things. In the midst of the chaos, a man waved me over.

"Are you two okay on your own?" I asked. I didn't want to run off and leave Eric and Angie to deal with these crazy fans alone.

"Yeah, we're fine. And he looks like some bigwig. Better run." Angie gave me a shove.

I walked over to the guy.

"You're the manager?" he asked. "We'd be really interested in having a chat with you. I think you'll be interested too."

He handed me a business card with the name of his record company on it. I didn't squeal out loud, but I did just a little bit in my heart.

"Call me during the week," he said, "and we'll set something up. I'm sure you'll want to celebrate tonight."

When I got back to the table, Eric and Angie both looked at me. I showed them the card.

"This is awesome," said Angie.

"It's just a card. It might come to nothing."

"You are the best manager we've ever had," said Eric. "We'd have never got anywhere with someone like that before. He'd have kicked us out the door."

"Well, if you guys hadn't played your arses off tonight, he'd have never been interested."

"And thank you, Angie. You really made it all happen. How did you get so many people here?"

Angie grinned.

Finally, the crowd died down. We had a box of money and pretty much no stock left. I began to understand why people loved business so much.

"Are you coming out for drinks with us?" Eric asked.

"Hells yeah," said Angie.

But I could see Dad and Frank waiting just outside the doors. I couldn't put that off.

Chapter 16

"It'd only be for a few days," Dad said. "It's not like it's a big deal."

"You're kidding, right? I can't believe you're asking me that."

I hugged the cash box to my chest. This was money I'd earned with my own sweat and brains. My precious money – well, some of it was my precious money. Most of it, of course, had to go to the band. But I had a nice cut of it just for me.

Not only had he got me to agree to him staying with me for a few days, Dad now wanted to borrow the money we'd made on the merchandise sales. When Dad realised I had a box full of cash, he'd come straight out and asked for it. He said he knew someone who could help him but he needed a few grand to tide him over. I could see his point – maybe he could use the money to get out of trouble – but I couldn't just give it to him like that.

Dad had settled down on a mattress on the floor. He had a small bag with him and not much else. He hadn't told me what he'd been doing since he left. I sat on the edge of my bed, removing my make-up.

I wanted to curl up in a little ball in my bed and have a good cry, but I couldn't even do that with Dad there. I had to pretend to be happy to see him. This room, with its crappy furniture, worn and stained by lifetimes of random strangers using it, the draught coming up through the cracks in the floorboards, the stains on the walls – it'd been barely as much as I could deal with when I thought it was just for a few weeks, but now, now I realised I'd be here much longer than that. There was no end in sight. I crumpled inside, as though I'd fallen into a big, black hole and the only way out was to scrape my way out inch by inch. There was no rescue team. I couldn't depend on Dad after all.

I'd always believed that Dad would return and, on that day, he'd have regained all his money and the house and the cars and my life. He'd come charging in and take me back to that life, handing me a fistful of bills to go shopping. All this poverty would dissolve away like the grime on my skin in the shower. I would never have to have another night of listening to the weird sounds of that house or worrying that I'd get home and find my door kicked in and all my stuff gone. I'd not have to catch the train and have to walk past that guy holding up the sign asking for money, the one who sat curled up with his clothes all turned to a sludgy grey. I'd not have to dress up in stupid costumes and hand out promotions to stupid, greedy people.

Instead he was in a worse position than me. Since he got back, he couldn't even meet my eyes when he talked, and instead of bellowing in roars of laughter that shook his whole body, he'd become quiet.

I threw the used make-up wipes in the bin and turned out the main light.

I couldn't sleep, though. All these emotions boiled up in me. Out there, my life, my real life, carried on without me in it. Like a soap opera when you missed a few episodes. My friends at uni got together for coffee and went to parties. Tom probably had a new girlfriend, because he sure as hell hadn't called me. There would be an empty desk in the exam room. It wasn't fair. I didn't deserve this life. My muscles quivered and my eyeholes prickled. It was okay for people who were born poor. They knew how to deal with it. I'd grown up not even knowing how to use a washing machine or cook two-minute noodles. I had no life skills. Then people laughed at me for not knowing stuff. I tried to choke back a sob.

"Are you okay, princess?"

Hearing him call me princess just made me want to sob more.

"What do you need the money for, anyway?"

"It's not that I don't want to tell you; you're just better off not knowing."

That didn't reassure me.

"I can't, Dad. If it was my money, I would in a heartbeat, but it's not."

He turned away from me and faced the wall. A lump rose up in my throat. I wasn't a princess any more. I was a girl who had nothing.

I had to put the cashbox somewhere while I slept. If I hid it, Dad would see where it was. A band squeezed tight around my chest. Did I really not trust my own father? He'd do anything for me. He always had. But the look in his eyes when he'd asked for the money scared me. It reminded me of the sludgy grey man outside the station. It wasn't that I didn't trust him; I just didn't want him to have that temptation around. I put the box in my bed. Just in case. If I slept with it in my arms, then I'd know where it was.

Dad still had his back to me but he wasn't asleep. I could tell by his breathing. It felt strange, having him sleeping in my room, yet familiar in a way. I'd almost drifted off to sleep when a flood of memories came rushing back. I didn't even know if they were real or just something I'd imagined.

"Dad, I want to know something? Dad?"

"Yeah?"

"When I was a kid, we went away somewhere, right?"

He turned slightly.

"Huh?"

"Somewhere in Asia, I think? We stayed with a man and you slept on my floor like this."

He turned but didn't answer me for a long time. Just when I'd given up trying to get an answer, he spoke.

"Yeah. After your mother died. I couldn't cope with things, and Harry got me to come and stay with him. What made you think of that now?"

So it was true.

But the dates didn't seem to match up. By my adding up, it didn't seem right. I'd been two years old when Mum died, but when we went away, I'd been in school.

"Where did we live before that? Where did we live with Mum?"

I tried to picture the house but all I had was a memory of a kitchen, a green-and-orange kitchen. On the top of the cupboard, she had a big brown jar that had cookies in it. Those cookies were mighty tasty. I'd look up at the jar, hoping she'd notice and hand me a cookie, and the whole kitchen smelled like cinnamon. That house had been small, with that nice, warm kitchen.

Then it turned cold without Mum, and I was on my own a lot. One day, I climbed up on the bench and got down that jar. If Mum wasn't around to give me a cookie, I'd get one myself. It took me so long to get the lid off the jar. It was on tight, or maybe I was just a weak little kid. Anyway, I finally got it off.

The cookie jar was empty. That's when I realised Mum wasn't around. She was gone. She'd never come back.

Then one night, Dad woke me up.

"Pack your stuff, princess. We're going on an adventure."

But it had scared me and I'd cried.

"Hush, princess. You have to be strong, stronger than anyone."

He went out and left me to pack. I put my teddy bear and my colouring-in books in the bag. Then I shoved in my pretty red shoes.

"Are you done, princess?" Dad asked when he came back to my room.

I nodded my head.

When I got outside, I shivered in the cold night air. Dad scooped me into his arms.

"I need my coat." Dad always remembered my coat.

"We don't have time, princess."

We sped through the dark to the airport, but I had no idea where we were going or why. I still didn't.

"Who was the man we stayed with?" I asked Dad, trying to figure this all out.

"Harry? A friend. You don't need to worry about him."

"And the woman? Pet-Lee? His wife?"

"Her name wasn't Pet-Lee. And she wasn't his wife. You called her Pet-Lee because you couldn't say her name properly. You shouldn't worry about these things now. Forget all about it. It was years ago."

She'd been so angry with Dad when she'd helped me unpack my case.

"She have no clothes? Only a teddy bear? No underwear?" the woman hissed at Dad. "Didn't you check her bag?"

Dad had shaken his head and not met her eyes.

The next day, Pet-Lee had taken me shopping. Not to a nice store but a big dusty market, with blurs of colour and sounds and smells I couldn't recognise. I clung to Pet-Lee's hand. She smiled and told me not to let go or I'd get lost in the crowd. Brown faces whizzed past up on motorbikes and people yelled so loud. I'd had to wear the pyjamas I'd had on when I left home and I got so hot, they stuck to my legs. When a man yelled at us in strange words, I started crying, so Pet-Lee took me to a stall and got me an iced drink. It tasted like sunshine and happy days. The ladies from the stall patted my hair and said I looked pretty, so that I forgot to cry.

Then we found the blue dress with white ruffles and bows and big puffy sleeves. I wanted it because it looked like the princess dresses in my books even though it felt scratchy. Pet-Lee bought it for me and I put it on straight away. The women put bows in my hair and I wanted to dance and twirl so that everybody knew I was a princess.

That's mainly what I remembered from that time. Dad was away a lot and I spent most of my time in the kitchen with Pet-Lee. He'd slept on a mattress on the floor in my room and he'd come in late at night and fall straight into bed and start snoring.

One night, Dad had come home and said we were leaving. Pet-Lee hugged me and cried. I cried too. When we came home, we moved into the big house in a different town. I started living a different life. I never even remembered until now that I'd left the blue dress behind.

It did seem odd when I thought about it. I'd never questioned how Dad had got his money or what happened in his business. After that, he'd been rich, it seemed. I had a maid to look after me, and everything I wanted.

Even when he'd disappeared, I'd believed he was innocent and it was all a misunderstanding. One day, he'd come back and explain it all. Now he was back and there were no explanations, just him wanting to borrow money. I wondered what had happened before, wondered if that's when this had all started.

I woke up the next day to someone banging on my door. I put the pillow over my head. They'd go away. The banging continued. Surely they'd go away. They had the wrong room, or they were someone I didn't want to see. Why wouldn't they stop?

Dad stirred in his sleep. Whoever was at the door kept banging, and if I didn't answer, they'd wake up the whole house.

I opened the door to see Jack Colt on my doorstep. Why was he there? When I'd left, he was off to some bar with the band. Surely he should be in bed, nursing a hangover with some slutty blonde next to him. Maybe the singer from that band. What the hell was he doing at my door, looking so bright-eyed?

He grinned at me, which threw me for a moment. The intense gaze of his brown eyes softened as the smile crinkled the corners.

"What's up?" I asked, rubbing my eyes and trying to focus. I didn't wake up easily. I probably looked a mess in my pink rabbit pyjamas and my bed hair.

"I thought I'd come and check on you. You took off so fast last night I didn't get to see you after the show. I wanted to thank you and see if you were okay."

I stared at him for a moment. This wasn't right. Had he been taken over by aliens? He seemed so nice and concerned. It took me a moment to register what he'd said. He was worried about me?

"I'm fine. I just had things to do."

The polite thing to do, I guess, would have been to invite him in, but that's kind of hard when you live in one room. One room that had gotten very messy, not to mention having a big lump of Dad in the middle of it.

He leaned on the door frame. "Well, if you want, I'll take you out to breakfast."

"Cool, I'll just chuck some clothes on. You wait out in the hallway."

I pushed the door closed.

I rummaged around the clothes pile, looking for a dress to throw on. Something that made me look incredibly hot yet as if I'd made no effort whatsoever. Should I put make-up on? Would that look like I was trying too hard? I didn't want to look as if I actually cared but I didn't want to look like a scuzzy mess either.

I found a cute dress that I knew hugged my curves and slipped it on.

"Who's at the door, honey?" Dad rolled over in his sleep, shielding his eyes.

"Just a friend," I said.

I heard angry footsteps in the hallway and ran out just in time to see the front door slam.

I ran out after him.

"Jack?" I called as he stormed off down the street.

What was up with him? Too bloody moody for my liking. Why was he asking me to breakfast, then taking off like he was in a big huff?

Then it dawned on me. He'd heard Dad's voice. Since he didn't know I had Dad staying with me, it must've looked like I'd picked up some random guy and brought him home. Surely he wouldn't think that? I'm not the type of girl who'd pick up some guy. And I'm definitely not that kind who'd go out to breakfast with one man while I still had another in my bed.

I ran after him in my bare feet but he'd gone so fast and the roughness of the concrete footpath cut into me. I wanted to explain to him. I wanted to see that happy, crinkly smile again that I'd seen a minute ago.

"Jack!" I called again but he was at the end of the street.

I figured I'd call him when I got inside and make him see reason. My side hurt a bit and I remembered the cashbox. I'd work out the band's share this morning and loan Dad what I could of mine. Maybe I'd been a bit harsh with him. We were family, after all, and we only had each other to depend on.

When I got back inside, I screamed.

Dad sat on my bed with the lid prised off the cashbox and a bundle of notes in his hand.

"What the hell are you doing?" I screamed. "Put that back."

I grabbed the money from him. My stomach burned and I wanted to throw up. Did I have no one in my life I could trust?

Dad hunched his shoulders and turned from me. He seemed to shrink away.

"Hon, I'll get it back to you in the next day or two. Trust me," he mumbled.

But any trust I'd felt dissolved. I couldn't even leave him alone for a few minutes.

"I said no. I love you, Dad, but I can't do this. I am just getting my stuff together. Don't mess it up for me." My voice shook but I had to say it. I swallowed hard and waited for him to apologise. I still believed that he could make this right.

"After all I've done for you," he said and shook his head.

I didn't even have the dream of Dad coming to rescue me now. All I had was lies and deceit and everything gone to shit. I had to get out of there. This hurt was too big for me to handle.

Chapter 17

The teller at the bank asked me what was wrong and I tried to stop crying but that just made the tears worse. I handed over the cashbox and got the receipt but didn't want to go back to my room. I wandered around the streets, wishing I had sunglasses to cover my eyes. I must have looked a mess. I walked and walked, not even knowing where I was going.

I had no idea what the time was or how long I'd walked, but the day got warmer and the sun got brighter. My shoes rubbed against my toes and my calves ached. I needed coffee and I needed food. I had to find a café somewhere so I could sit quietly by myself and think about how to work this out.

When I walked into the café, I scanned the place for somewhere quiet to sit – a nice corner table where I didn't have to deal with people. Instead of finding that, I saw Jack Colt sitting at a table near the door. Was he stalking me? I ran out of the café and on to the street, but he followed me out.

"Are you okay?" he asked. "You look a mess."

I tried to reply but started crying again and he wrapped his arms around me. He didn't talk or ask me what was wrong. He just held me.

Every time I thought I'd finished, that I'd cried all the tears I could cry, a fresh sob rose in my throat and I clutched him tighter. If I let go, I'd have been set adrift in the world, but he anchored me and made me feel like I could deal with anything so long as he held me in his arms. I'd never had a pair of strong arms to hold me when I'd been upset before. I'd never had anyone to just let me feel the things I needed to feel without telling me to be strong.

Finally the tears stopped. I'd saturated Jack's shoulder and I felt spent from all the crying.

"I think you need food," he said.

"And coffee." I sobbed the words out but I felt better. I'd cried enough.

We went back into the café and sat down. I ordered the large breakfast with extra toast and extra bacon. Suddenly, I felt like I could eat all the food in the world and still be hungry.

"It was my dad. At my place this morning."

He screwed up his face for a moment, then nodded.

"Is that why you left? Because you heard his voice?"

"No, not at all." But he said it funny and I thought he was lying. He'd been pissed off, for sure. Maybe a little bit jealous. He wouldn't have stormed out like that unless he felt something. The thought that he might be jealous made me feel a bit happier.

I took a slice of his toast while I waited for my food to arrive.

"So, last night, huh? Wasn't it something?"

He nodded, then reached over to brush my hair out of my eyes. I stole a glance at him and wondered why he did that. It seemed so intimate. I noticed his fingers, so long and thin. Perfect for playing guitar. I noticed his forearm with the black tattoo, the hairs on his arm lit up by the sun coming through the window. I noticed the way his t-shirt stretched across his chest. I noticed gold streaks in his eyes.

"Why are you staring at me?"

"Am not," I said and picked up the newspaper. "I'm so not staring at you."

Then my food arrived. I gulped down the eggs and bacon and tomato like I'd never seen food before and never once looked up at Jack Colt, even though I could feel him looking at me. This relationship was strictly business. If his t-shirt emphasised his strong shoulders and that incredibly sexy V where they met the top of his arm, that wasn't anything. Just one more thing to sell the band. I had no interest whatsoever.

Then I remembered he owed me.

"So, you were going to tell me your dark secret," I said. "You lost the bet."

He laughed, but I insisted.

"It's not something I like to talk about." He grabbed a slice of toast off my plate and looked at me as if daring me to say anything. I didn't care. My stomach was so full, I never wanted to eat again.

"Well, obviously. It'd be no point having a bet about something you went around telling the world."

"The warehouse belongs to my father. My biological father. I don't have anything to do with him, but he gives me money sometimes and thinks that's enough."

I choked on my coffee. I'd been thinking I was the rich bitch, but now I had nothing and Jack Colt had all the money.

"So, what's the story? You give me shit about being a rich girl who's slumming it, but really it's you that's doing that?"

He leaned forward, resting his elbows on the table.

"My mum came from a poor family and they met when they were young. It was a love-at-first-sight thing. You know, the whole young love with hearts and flowers and everything was going to be perfect so long as they were together."

"But it didn't last?"

I sipped at my coffee while he stared out the window.

"They were fine at first. But shit like that, it never lasts. People think they are all in love and they can overcome any obstacle. Then the obstacles are there, day after day, and the love isn't as strong as it used to be."

He'd grabbed a sugar sachet and twisted it in his hands.

"But surely you can work through those things, talk them over?"

He snorted. "You think?"

"Yeah, I really do think. If you really want it to work." I don't even know where I'd gotten ideas like that. I mean, Dad had never had a relationship that I knew about since Mum died, and my only serious relationship, with Tom, had died when it became no longer convenient.

"Whatever. She got knocked up with me and he gave her a fistful of cash to deal with it."

"What did she do?"

He stopped to sip his coffee. I wondered how he felt about all this. He tried to sound detached, but at times his voice shook, and he'd twisted the sugar sachet so much, it'd split and the sugar spilt on the table.

"She moved back home to Gran's, and Gran pretty much raised me. Mum wasn't around much. She had boyfriends. I lost count of them. They were all no-good scum, the whole lot of them. She'd think she was in love. *He's the one, he's the one*, is what she'd say. Until he was another lying, cheating douchebag."

He stopped again. His eyes clouded over like he was no longer there but off somewhere I couldn't reach.

"I got home from school one day. I was fourteen at the time, and there was an ambulance outside Gran's house. I wanted to run then, run as fast as I could, so I didn't have to go inside. But I sucked it up, you know. Gran had had a heart attack. They got her out of there and into hospital. I couldn't even contact Mum. Didn't know where she was."

He still held the fragments of the sugar packet in his clenched fist. I reached out and put my hand over his. He didn't seem to notice, but he didn't shake it off either.

"She was a tough old bird, but she'd been old when Mum was born. No one lasts forever. I went in to see her every day and then, at the end, had to make all the arrangements myself. I had to move out of her place, of course, but had nowhere else to go. Mum'd shacked up with some loser at the time and he sure as hell didn't want me around. I lived where I could – friend's couches, squats, sometimes sleeping outside. I started playing guitar around then. One of the friends I stayed with had one that was gathering dust in the corner."

"You taught yourself?"

He nodded.

"Pretty much. I moved back into the squat, but the council was coming down hard on that kinda stuff back then. I got kicked out and most of my stuff got broken or stolen. I'd never wanted to take anything from my father, but I had no choice. Some guy turned up with an offer and I was sick of doing it rough. I moved into the warehouse and met Eric not long after that. Mum's still pretty messed up, though. I dunno. I help her out when I can."

That woman we'd seen. Was that his mother? Angie and I had joked about it, but we'd not considered the possibility she really was.

We ordered another coffee. I wanted to reach out and hug him, but his face changed in an instant. No more sad eyes. No more unhappy Jack.

"And that's the hard-luck story of Jack Colt. Do you think it'll sell?"

I gulped. I didn't want to seem callous, but I thought it would.

"Do you keep in touch with your dad?" I probably knew him. This wasn't such a big town.

Jack laughed, but bitterly this time.

"I don't even know who he is. Mum won't talk about him. Everything I know, I learnt from Gran, and she never told Gran either. He handled everything through a lawyer. Probably didn't want me chasing him for more money or something. The only thing I have is this."

He pulled out a chain from under his shirt. It had a ring on it. A man's ring. It had an insignia that looked like a bird. Before I could see any more, he tucked it away.

"He gave that to Mum, but Gran hid it away and gave it to me. She said Mum would just hock it for cash to give to one of her loser boyfriends otherwise. It doesn't have much meaning, but I kept it because Gran told me to."

If it didn't mean anything, why did he bother wearing it?

"So, what about you?"

I told him a bit about what had happened. Not the part about Dad trying to steal the money, though. Not about that.

"Things must have been tough for you the past few months, huh?"

I nodded. "But they're looking up now. Did Eric tell you about the record company guy?"

"Yeah, that's fantastic."

"Except for parents." I sighed. I did not want to go home and face my dad. I couldn't bear looking at what he'd become. Maybe he'd been like that all along and I'd just never seen it. He'd never been so desperate before.

"So, do you have plans for today? We're rehearsing. Wanna come along?"

I grinned. Sounded perfect to me.

Chapter 18

I never knew hanging around rehearsal would be so much fun. I thought it'd be annoying with them going over and over the same bits of songs – and it was a bit – but then Jack would play something that sounded like nothing at all. Just some random notes. Then he'd play some more and the others would join in and suddenly it became *something*. The three of them worked together to create music out of nothing, as though they had one brain and one soul.

"Hey, manager," Jack said. "Why are you lazing around on the sofa?"

I'd parked myself on a couch, thumbing through a magazine while they played. That suited me fine, staying on the periphery.

"I'm working. This is my job."

"Get your butt up here, we need someone on the tambourine."

I thought he was kidding until a tambourine flew through the air and landed on my chest with a twinkling thud.

"That hurt."

"Come on, get up here."

"Yeah, get up here," added Eric.

This was totally embarrassing. What did I know about playing a tambourine? I'd only make a fool of myself. The couch was plenty good enough for me. But Jack and Eric grabbed my arms and pulled me up.

"Okay, okay. I'll do it and prove to you I'm crap."

I started shaking the tambourine around. Jack grabbed me from behind and guided my movements. It didn't seem that hard but I wasn't in any hurry to let on. Maybe it was my imagination, but he did seem to get himself into situations that involved putting his arms around me quite a lot.

The heat of his body warmed my back and I could almost feel his heartbeat. His hand covered mine, prompting me when to tap the tambourine and when to shake it. His other hand rested on my waist. His breath tickled my neck and my heart felt lighter. I tried not to grin too much but to focus on his movements.

As Spud began tapping the drums, we followed his beat – shake, shake, tap. That was easy but, as the beat became faster, we both moved, our hips swaying in time. Shake, shake, tap. And a hip thrust on the tap.

I leaned back against him and maybe my thrusts became a bit more of a grind. He responded by grinding himself into me and pulling me a bit tighter into him. Then suddenly he pulled away from me.

"Right, let's do 'Party Dress,' from the top."

Spud started with the drums, a simple beat leading in. I followed what he was doing. Soon, I got the hang of it and was playing along with them. I shook my hips and tapped the tambourine against them. I looked at Jack and he grinned back at me. A thrill went through me. I was really doing this.

I felt at one, not just with Jack but with the entire band. I'd worked with them to create this. I bit my bottom lip to control my smile but it was something awesome, this teamwork thing.

I didn't even need to concentrate, I began moving around, doing some sexy little dance moves, shaking my hips and running my free hand down my body.

Then I thought I'd do some backup vocals, singing along with the melody.

"Stop! Stop!" Jack seemed distressed. Had his amp blown a fuse? He'd stopped playing.

All three of them stared at me.

"What's wrong?" I asked.

"Your singing..."

Was I really that good? They did seem awestruck. Maybe I could do this, maybe I could have my own singing career. I'd always thought I'd look great up onstage.

"Yeah, sorry, Hannah, but that's really putting me off." Eric smiled at me apologetically.

"I've heard strangled cats sound better," added Spud.

"You're joking, right?" I could sing. I could sing really well. People had always said so. They were just having a joke.

"NO!" all three of them cried.

"It's terrible." Jack shook his head as though he couldn't believe what he'd just heard.

I picked up a cushion from the couch and threw it at Jack. Then I picked up another and threw it at Eric.

Jack and Eric looked at each other, then rushed at me with the cushions, raining blows down on me. I covered my head to block them. They knocked me back onto the couch as I tried to wrench the cushions from their hands.

"Stop, stop." I tried to sound serious but I couldn't stop laughing.

Instead of stopping, Jack went for my ribs, tickling me until I screamed. I tried to squirm away from him but rolled onto the floor. He kept at it, pinning me down so I had no control. His fingers dug into my ribs again and I squirmed and screamed until I fell on the floor in exquisite agony. Even that didn't stop him, though. If anything, it seemed to encourage him. He straddled me and kept tickling. I kicked out with my legs and punched at him, trying to get him off me, feeling as if I'd pee my pants.

Then he stopped and looked down at me. His hair flopped in his eyes and his face was flushed. He relaxed his grip on my wrists and I could've easily rolled out from under him while his guard was down, but I no longer wanted to.

Everything else stopped until it became just the two of us in the entire world. Every part of me became aware of him, moving closer to me as though in slow motion. I bucked my hips, not wanting to get away, but wanting to feel his body against mine.

His gaze went from my face to my nipples, hard and straining against the thin fabric of my dress. So hard that they almost caused me pain. I wanted to feel his full lips pressed around them, sucking and licking.

"Hey, settle down, you two. Get a room."

Well, that sure broke the spell. I'd forgotten about the other two in the studio but became fully aware of my surroundings and the floor beneath me, and the hard cock of Jack Colt pressing into my leg.

"Huh?" Jack turned to Spud.

"Are we rehearsing or are the two of you just going to fool around?" Spud looked really angry. "We're renting this space by the hour, remember, so if you want to fool around, leave it for after rehearsal."

Jack jumped up.

"I guess we should get back to work."

I stayed on the ground for a moment, shell-shocked. What had just happened? Eric shot me a look that I couldn't figure out and Jack didn't look at me at all.

"Hannah, pull your dress down," Spud said. "You look like a dirty whore."

I gave Spud a withering look.

"You don't have to be so crass." I smoothed my dress down, but I was pretty sure that it hadn't been up around my waist or anything. I tried to catch Jack's eye, even Eric's, so they could back me up.

I bet Spud just wished he'd been the one pinned down by Jack instead.

Spud shrugged.

"Come on, Jack," he said. "Balls to the wall. Forget the distractions and let's rock."

Jack straightened his shirt and ran his fingers through his hair before picking up his guitar.

I figured they didn't need me around to watch them play. I picked up my bag and waved them goodbye.

Chapter 19

You know when you wake up feeling like a prizefighter has used your body as a punching bag for a workout session during the night? Yeah, that.

I couldn't move. I seriously could not move. I tried to lift my head off the pillow but I didn't have the strength. I didn't have the motivation either because it was as cold as an iceberg out there. I wouldn't have been surprised to see a penguin waddling through the room.

My legs, my back, my arms. My throat. Had I been swallowing razor blades? I couldn't remember doing that, yet that's what my throat felt like. I pulled the blankets up; I'd just stay there and die, or at least try to get my strength back. Bed wasn't warm but it was warmer than it was out there.

Then I remembered, I had to get up and do stuff. I'd promised Angie I'd meet her at the station. I had no time for lollygagging around in bed.

But, that cold, draughty train station concourse and standing there for two hours. And now we weren't even snuggled up in nice warm tree frog costumes but cutesy '60s-style air hostess uniforms. The wind would whip around my legs until I shivered myself to death.

I tried to stand up and move to the bathroom but, as soon as my feet hit the floor, I felt dizzy. And the draught came through the floorboards, wrapping my feet in chilling fingers like a monster trying to drag me to its subarctic hell.

I scrambled for the socks I'd kicked off in my sleep. My pink-and-white bed socks I'd gotten for only two dollars. I put them on. But the tiles in the bathroom would be even colder than the floor in my room. I didn't have the mental strength to deal with that cold. The pressure building up in my face made it hard for me to think. My temples throbbed and everything looked blurry.

Surely they didn't want a bleary-eyed, hollow shell of a promo girl handing out their stuff? If I looked half as bad as I felt, people would flee from me in terror.

I put my feet back under the covers and tried to find the warm spot in the bed, then lunged out for my bag, using a magazine to knock it closer so I didn't have to get out from the bed. I hooked the magazine around the strap and lifted it to me. Hannah ingenuity.

My phone wasn't in my bag, though. I'd set it somewhere after I'd called Frank the night before.

I'd gotten home in a decent mood, despite Spud being a pissy little bitch at the rehearsal. My anger with Dad had gone and I'd thought out a plan on the way home. We could work out how much money he needed and I'd scrape up as much as I could. I had my share of the band money and the leftover from selling my clothes. I'd offer that to him. After all, he was family and I had to help out.

When I opened the door, though, I couldn't see any sign of Dad.

"Dad?" I called out, even though it was hardly like he'd be hiding under the bed or in the dresser. "Dad?"

He might have gone out for the day but I looked for his bag and couldn't find it.

He'd gone to Frank's. That had to be it. He'd figured he'd stay there until I cooled off.

I rang Frank.

"Is Dad there?"

"I haven't heard from him since last night. Why?"

"He's not here. We had a disagreement this morning." That was an understatement but I didn't want to spill it all out to

Frank. "I've been out all day and now he's not here and his bag has gone too."

There was a long silence, then Frank spoke.

"Shit, Hannah. That's not good. That's not good at all. That's really messed things up... no, no, it's not your fault... it's just, we could've worked something out."

Stupid Frank, being all cryptic again. Now I had no Dad, just a horrible tight feeling in my chest, making me think I'd been a real bitch to him.

The whole Dad issue could go on the back burner until I had the brain capacity to deal. I had no idea if he was even still around or if he'd run back to where he'd been hiding. I hadn't asked him about that. I hadn't really talked to him much about his life because I'd been so angry. Now, the thought of it all made my head more blurry.

Phone, phone, where are you, phone?

There was so much junk beside my bed, though – coffee cups and magazines and a book Angie had loaned me and three things of eye shadow, including purple, and I never even knew I owned a purple eye shadow.

I needed to clean up this pigsty but I lacked the strength. I wanted to go back to sleep but I couldn't until I'd called Angie.

I lifted the magazine. Yay! Phone.

I rang Angie and told her I couldn't make it.

"I'm sorry, you'll just have to promo without me. The show must go on and all that..." Then I started coughing like an old man.

"Just get well. I'll be stuck in the edit suite at school for hours after that but I'll pop around when I've finished to check on you. Do you need anything? Juice? Soup? Trashy magazines?"

"Yes. All of the above. And coffee. I don't even think I can make it to the coffee shop."

Angie laughed and hung up while I collapsed back into bed. She was the best. I could not even conceive of trying to get out of bed to go to the shops.

I needed to get up and turn the heater on and maybe get some more blankets. I needed another pair of socks on my feet and some gloves. But the socks were so far away. I'd nap first to gather my strength.

I must have napped all day because I woke up to the phone ringing and the deep shadows of late afternoon in my room. I'd only woken up to cough and hack and feel miserable before falling back to sleep again.

Where'd I put that phone after I'd used it? I could hear the muffled ring. It wasn't on the floor. It kept ringing and finally I found it, under the blankets.

Angie?

But it was Jack Colt. He talked some stuff but I couldn't really follow him. He talked something... something... record company guy... something. His words blurred in my head and didn't make any sense.

"Huh?" Then I started hacking again.

"You sound like shit."

"Yeah, well, I feel like shit too. I think I'm dying." My voice croaked out like a broken thing.

"I'll come over."

Before I could tell him no, he'd hung up. I didn't want Jack Colt to come over. If I sounded like shit and felt like shit, chances were I looked like shit too and I lacked the strength to put on make-up. Maybe I could get a scarf and wrap it around my face. I'd just have to suck it up and let him see me looking like a monster because I really could not move.

Not long after that, he knocked on my door.

"Wow, you really look like shit!"

"Thanks." I sat on the edge of the bed, shivering. I rubbed my arms to get some warmth in them. The room had gotten even colder. I'd put on a hat and some gloves and wore about five layers of clothes but that didn't help. I had three pairs of socks on my feet.

Jack wrapped a blanket around me and put his hand against my forehead.

"You're burning up. You're really sick. Do you have any cold tablets?"

I shook my head and pulled the blanket around me tighter. Even though he said I was hot, I felt freezing cold. He put his arm around me and stroked my hair. That made me feel a bit better, the feeling of his hand on my hair. Comforting, yet at the same time thrilling. I didn't even want to think about the tingles he sent through me when he did that. Not when I felt so sick.

I leaned my head on his shoulder and let him caress me. I couldn't remember anyone ever being so gentle and caring, not even when I was a child. I'd always been told I was fine and to be tough. But it was nice, for just a few minutes, to let him look after me.

I could try not being tough and not being fine but just letting him soothe me. The softness of his jumper tickled my cheek. It felt cosy and warm. Something stirred in my stomach. Not the crappy sick feeling I'd had all day but something warm and nice.

Then my nose started running. I didn't want to move to get a tissue in case it distracted him and the spell he'd created got broken, but I couldn't sit there with snot dripping down my face either. Who even wants a guy to see her like that? All the glamour I tried to surround myself with had disappeared and I was just a sick and snotty girl. I tried to sniff quietly so he wouldn't notice. Just a few short, gentle sniffs. Maybe I'm a gross person, but who'd move in that position?

That didn't even help. I'd become a factory of mucus and phlegm. A dripping tap.

He reached across me and pulled a tissue out of the box, his arm leaning across my lap. I sucked in my breath, not sure how to act with him that close to me. He handed the tissue to me.

"Now, blow!" He said it in a strict voice.

He pushed me back on the bed and wiped my nose, as if I was a little kid or something. I tried to push him off so I could do it myself but he had me down firm.

"What the hell are you doing?"

Angie stood in the middle of the room with a bag of groceries in one hand and a coffee in the other. She hadn't knocked, so I must've not shut the door properly after Jack came in. She stared at Jack and at me. Her eyes flashed cold, as if she wanted me dead. I could see that from her point of view it must've looked bad, the two of us frolicking on the bed.

"Looks like you don't need me." She threw the bag of groceries on the floor and ran out.

"Angie, Angie... don't go."

But it was too late. I tried to follow her but my legs quivered like jelly. I collapsed back onto the bed, but I needed to explain to her. I'd told her I wasn't interested in Jack, and I wasn't. I really wasn't. It was just that he was so soft and lovely. I'd thought she just had a fangirl crush on Jack, nothing serious, but from the crumpled look on her face when she'd seen us, maybe she liked him a lot more than she'd let on.

A lump rose in my throat with worry that she hated me now. She'd sure looked as if she hated me when she ran out. If she'd been one of my friends, my old friends from my old life, I'd have laughed and felt superior to them, but this was Angie. I really wanted her to like me. I wanted her to think I was a good person. I liked it when we hung out together. We were a team.

I sobbed a little, a strangled cry from my heart.

Jack looked at me, quizzically.

"What was that about?"

"Forget about it. Girl stuff." I didn't want to explain and I didn't know if Angie wanted me going into all the details of her feelings. If Jack hadn't worked that out for himself, then I wasn't about to tell him.

He shrugged.

"Okay, but you can't stay here. This place is like a bloody freezer. Come over to our place so you can recover. We have central heating and you'd have decent food."

I shook my head. That would only make things worse with Angie.

"I'm not taking no for an answer. I can't leave you here like this." He put his arm around me and lifted me off the bed. I really had no choice. Not without telling him, and then he'd think I was stupid for even imagining that he felt anything for me.

"My phone." I could contact Angie to explain. Surely she'd not even think anyone was interested in me when I looked like a red-faced, snotty-nosed pig.

He sat me down and tidied up the groceries Angie had dropped. I really wished she'd given me my coffee before she took off.

I grabbed my phone and made sure I had the necessities in my bag – wallet, keys and lip balm.

He reached for me again.

"It's okay, I can walk to the car."

I pulled the blanket around myself and shuffled outside.

In the car, I tried to call Angie but she didn't answer her phone. Then I tried to send her a text but it was hard to find the words. What did I say? *I know you like Jack and you think we were up to something but it was not what it looked like.* That sounded a bit weird but it was the best I could do. It took me the whole drive just to write that and then rewrite it.

Jack put me to bed and I snuggled under the blankets, feeling warm for the first time that day. Why had he changed so much? From the snarly horrible beast that ignored me, to this gentle man who looked after me when I was sick? Maybe he had multiple personalities? That seemed like the most likely explanation. I'd seen a movie once with someone like that. I shouldn't overthink it, anyway, just appreciate the warm bed and the care. It sure beat being in my lousy flat, shivering to death with no food.

As I drifted off to sleep, I could hear the gentle strumming of a guitar from downstairs. That soothed me too and made me feel the same as when Jack stroked my hair. I smiled as I feel asleep.

I woke up in a dark room with everything totally still. I had no idea what time it was but I figured it was the middle of the night. I felt for my phone so I could check the time. I had a feeling like I'd forgotten about something awful. It clawed around in my belly like a frightened animal, scratching and seething. I tried to remember.

Angie. She'd been so mad.

I switched on my phone to check for messages.

Nothing.

She must've been really mad. Angie checked her phone like every two minutes. She never missed a call. And it was two a.m. She wouldn't be calling back any time soon. I felt a bit better and wide awake. I didn't want to get up and disturb Jack, who must be sleeping on the couch again, or Eric, so I stared at the ceiling, trying to figure things out.

If I'd stayed at school, I'd be starting exams that week. That really freaked me out. I'd learnt more in the last few weeks than I ever had at uni, but it wasn't the kind of stuff that helped you pass exams. I hadn't heard from Tom for ages either. Maybe he'd heard the rumours about Dad, or he was too busy studying for his law exams to even notice I wasn't there. I hadn't thought about him either. He'd been my boyfriend for four years but it was like he'd been a pretend boyfriend. I'd never felt that thrill when he kissed me. I'd not even known that kind of thrill was possible. Tom's kisses had the flavour of merging our companies together.

A taste of business partnerships and financial transactions. Jack's kisses, on the other hand, were like jumping on the back of a motorbike and heading out to somewhere unknown with the wind whipping through your hair. I'd seen that in a movie too, because I'd never been on a motorbike. Maybe I could buy one. Maybe that was the new me.

I needed a drink of water. I really needed a drink. I thought there would be one by my bed but there wasn't. If Jack wanted to play nurse, he could've brought me one. Even housekeepers knew how to do that. But then they leave and don't hold you or stroke your hair.

I tried to curl up and go back to sleep but all I could think of was having a cold glass of water. My throat felt so dry. If I didn't get out of bed and hydrate myself, I'd never get to sleep.

I tiptoed downstairs, not wanting to wake Jack. He slept on the couch, snoring a little. He'd breathe in a huge breath, then, when he exhaled, he made this funny little half-snore, half-snort sound. He lay half-turned towards the back of the couch, and his hair had flopped onto his face but wavered with each breath out. It looked so funny. Then I realised I was watching him sleep like some creepy creep.

His toes stuck out the bottom of the blanket. Even though the room was warm, I felt bad for those toes. He had long toes, just like his fingers, and the little one slightly twisted. I'd just tuck them in under the blanket.

I tiptoed around the couch, making sure not to wake him, and reached over to pull down the blanket, when I knocked the remote control off the coffee table. It crashed onto the floor, causing a huge echo through the still apartment.

Jack jumped off the couch and sprang at me. He grabbed my arm, all pent-up energy about to unfurl. Pain shot up through my shoulder.

"Jack! Don't."

I stumbled backwards, trying to untwist my arm and lessen the pain. I choked back screams, not wanting to startle him, but my pulse raced like crazy, the banging of my heart pounding my body.

He advanced towards me, his fingers squeezing tighter around my arm, bending it back. If he twisted it any more, it might snap. Who was this guy? Not the same person who'd held me so gently earlier.

I froze, not able to react.

"Jack, Jack," I pleaded, but this wasn't Jack.

His fist flew at me. I screamed.

That seemed to bring him to his senses.

He dropped his arm before the punch connected and he let go of me.

"What the hell are you doing?" he asked. I couldn't see his face clearly in the dim light, but his voice sounded shaky.

"I... I need some water."

"Oh, okay. I just thought... never mind." He sat down on the edge of the couch, his head in his hands. I wondered what was going on. He ran his fingers through his hair, then reached over and lit up a cigarette. In the glow of the cigarette, his eyes looked haunted.

"Are you okay?" I sat down beside him and tried to put my arm around him but he twisted away from me.

I waited but he didn't answer. He didn't react at all. It was as if he hadn't heard me or had forgotten I was there. The need to cough tickled at my throat but I suppressed it, not wanting to disturb him.

Eventually, I stood up and got a glass of water, then went back to bed. I felt so useless, as if I should've done something to help, but I had no idea what. Jack obviously wanted to close himself off from me, from everyone, and unless he let me in, I could do nothing.

I could hear him move around downstairs. He'd come so close to hitting me. Well not me. I don't think he had any idea who I was; it was someone else he saw in the dark. There was a lot I didn't know about Jack Colt, dark places that maybe I didn't want to know.

I checked my phone again and there were still no messages. Not that I expected one in the middle of the night. I lay awake for a long time, wondering what my life had become.

Chapter 20

The next morning, Eric woke me up with a cup of herbal tea.

"This will make you feel better," he said.

"Is it some wacky Asian medicine?" I sniffed the cup just in case it had some weird shit in it.

He wrinkled his forehead and then shook his head. "It's not Asian. It's honey and lemon. What? You think because I'm half-Korean, everything I do is some kind of Asian thing? Don't pigeonhole me, Hannah."

Before I could apologise, I noticed the grin on his face. I wrapped my hands around the cup, wanting to absorb its warmth. Eric sat on my bed and I told him about Jack.

"Oh, you should never wake up Jack when he's sleeping. He might kill you."

"You aren't joking about that. He was really freaked."

"There are some demons in that man's sleep that I'd hate to even know about," said Eric.

"You tell me that now," I said and laughed nervously. I wished I'd never gone near him.

"When we're on tour, we always make sure he has his own room."

"What? Spud doesn't spoon with him?"

We both laughed.

"You know he's got a girlfriend."

My heart sank. It sank right through the ground.

"Jack?" I asked in a strangled voice.

"No. Spud."

"No way. A girl girlfriend? But he's gay, right?" I sat up straighter. I needed details.

"Not gay."

"He's gay for Jack."

Eric grinned. "That may be so."

"Does he make her dress up as Jack during sex? I bet he does. Though I guess that would be safer..."

"There's shit that happened in Jack's life. He doesn't talk about it, but he lived on the streets for a while and I think he still doesn't feel safe at times."

"Oh yeah, before his dad bought him this place."

Eric's eyes widened and he laughed. I have no idea why. It didn't seem particularly funny to me.

"Did he tell you that story?"

I nodded.

"Jack's a strange one." Eric shook his head with a weird smile on his face. "Drink up your tea and you can sleep some more."

"Maybe I should leave today. I'm feeling better. I can look after myself."

Eric felt my temperature.

"You're still pretty feverish. Stay here. At least you know now."

I sunk back down into the bed and thought about what Eric had said. I was sure Jack would come up later and apologise and laugh the whole thing off.

I woke up to the smell of wonderful food. Spicy, garlicky smells. I'd barely eaten anything in the previous few days. I felt as if I could eat a horse. A huge horse. I jumped out of bed and headed downstairs.

Eric stirred something at the stove.

"Ah, you're awake. Do you want a shower?"

To be honest, I did feel pretty manky. I probably smelt a bit manky too. That was probably his way of saying I stunk.

"Sure, but I don't have a change of clothes or anything." I really didn't feel like putting my horrible old clothes back on. I'm pretty sure I'd sweat through them all.

"That's okay, I can loan you some pyjamas. They have a drawstring so you can tighten them to fit."

Eric ran off and returned with some neatly folded PJs and a towel.

"There's shampoo and everything in the bathroom. Help yourself."

I couldn't believe how good it felt to get under the warm water and wash all the sweat and grime from myself. I washed my hair and scrubbed myself clean. When I got out, I dried my hair and wished I had some make-up to put on. I looked through the cupboards. No cosmetics, as you'd expect, but they did have some high-quality skincare.

When I came out, Eric had set the food on the table. Huge bowls of soup. I'd be almost totally cured after eating that soup, I knew it. My stomach rumbled and I wished Eric would stop fussing around so we could sit down to eat.

Then I noticed there were only two bowls of soup.

"Where's Jack?"

Eric shrugged. "He's gone out. Didn't say where he's going."

I started eating. My mouth nearly exploded from the hot chillies and I grabbed for a glass of water.

Eric laughed. "I didn't know you couldn't handle the hot stuff."

"I can handle it. I can handle it fine. I just wasn't expecting it. I'm fine now. See? See?" I spooned the soup into my mouth and tried my hardest not to grimace at the spiciness of it.

Eric was such a good cook. No wonder, with a mother like he had. He also seemed to work hard at his graphics outside of the band. Altogether, he'd make a good boyfriend for someone. Not for me, obviously, since it'd be not right for me to date someone from the band, and I really did not want a boyfriend. But he'd make a great boyfriend for Angie. Better than Jack. She just had to see past Jack's rock star glamour and notice Eric's good points.

"How are you feeling now?"

"Much better. You and Jack have been so lovely, looking after me and letting me stay here. I must've been a mess yesterday."

"Yeah, Jack was really worried about you."

That made my stupid heart skip a beat.

"So," Eric said, "what do you want to do after dinner? We could watch a DVD or something."

"Sounds perfect."

I helped him clear up, then he got me a selection of DVDs to pick from. I expected guy movies, *Fast and Furious*-type things, or maybe music-type movies.

"So, who owns the chick flicks?"

Eric hung his head. He tried to look shamefaced but his mouth twitched at the corners.

"You big softie. Hey, what's this? *Busty, Horny Babes*?"

"Whaaaaat?" Eric jumped to grab the case out of my hand.

"Got you. You really believed it was, though, didn't you? You totally fell into my trap. How many horny babe DVDs do you own?"

"Hey, I thought it could've been Jack's. Of course it wouldn't have been mine."

"Yeah, you are more the kind of guy who has his porn on the computer, right?"

I laughed and he slapped at me.

We curled up on the couch. I grabbed one of the blankets sitting on the floor and put it over my legs. It smelt of Jack.

"This is cosy, isn't it?"

Eric set a big bowl of M&Ms down on the coffee table.

"I hope it doesn't put me in the friend zone." He gave me a lingering look, so that I had to break his gaze.

Was something going on there? Had Jack gone out and left us alone on purpose? I wasn't sure I liked that idea.

"Are we going to watch this or what?" I asked. Better to deflect comments like that than try to answer.

In the end, he'd convinced me to watch some Korean drama. I didn't care. Anything to just veg out on the couch was fine in my book. It was a bit of a pain to read the subtitles at first, but after the first episode, I really had to watch the next one to see what would happen.

"It's so predictable," I said. "The dumb girl is going to end up with the badass guy, isn't she?"

"So, you don't want to watch any more?"

"Hell yeah, I want to watch more. It's like crack cocaine."

He laughed.

"The evil chick might be evil, but she has the best hair. And the best clothes. I'd totally date the evil chick. Would I look good with that hair?"

Eric nodded and grabbed a handful of M&Ms.

"And the nice guy, he has really good cheekbones. She should totally pick him. He has better genes for babies."

"Is that important?"

"Hey, no one wants an ugly baby."

Our laughter got cut short by a crash at the door. Jack was home. I could smell the whiskey on him before he even got into the room. Then I heard a high-pitched giggle.

A woman in a tatty red fake-fur coat followed him in. She had hair that had been bleached to a strawy frizz, and red lipstick smudged across her mouth.

"Oh, Jack, there are people here," she shrieked as she came into the room. "Hope I'm not disturbing anything."

She threw herself on the chair, her legs flopping over the arm.

"Get me something to drink, will ya?"

I sat up straight on the couch. Jack came over and sat on the other arm of her chair, putting his arm around her.

My stomach spun out of control, like I was going to be sick. I didn't know who she was, but they were obviously very close. All that time he'd been looking after me and making sure I was okay, he'd just been being nice, obviously. Probably making sure that

I'd be well enough to call the record company guy and get down to business. If this woman was his type, he must have no interest in me because I was nothing like her at all. She reeked of cheap perfume mixed with booze and bad fashion.

Eric had sat up straight too, obviously feeling awkward with them.

"Eh, what's this shit?" She grabbed the remote off the coffee table and turned the DVD off. "Put on some music. You guys need to learn to party. We need something loud."

"We were watching that," said Eric in a soft voice, but she ignored him. He exchanged glances with me, rolling his eyes.

Jack went into the kitchen and returned with two glasses of red wine, handing her one.

"Aren't you guys drinking?"

She spun around to look at us, slopping red wine on the floor as she moved. The muscles in Eric's face spasmed just slightly. Not enough that anyone else noticed but me.

Jack leaned over, resting his arm on her shoulder. She stroked his leg and whispered something in his ear. They both giggled.

Now they were really making me sick. She play-slapped him.

"Oh, Jack, you shouldn't say things like that." She looked at me as if to imply they were talking about me.

I tried to ignore her and talk to Eric but could barely speak over the sound of her screeching laugh. She'd kicked her shoes off and her skirt had ridden up her legs so that she was practically showing her underwear.

"Can you call for a cab?" I asked Eric. "I think I need to go home."

"You don't have to. I'm sorry for that." He looked over at the chick.

"No need for you to apologise." I smiled at him. "You've been wonderful, cooking me dinner and watching dramas with me."

Eric smiled and gave me that strange look again.

"Yo, Hannah, get me a top-up, will you?" Jack held his wine glass out to me. "You're our manager, after all. You should earn your keep."

I gave him a withering look, but he just laughed. It was like he was going out of his way to be as obnoxious to me as he possibly could.

"Yeah, me too." The blonde laughed.

I stood up.

"I'll go outside and get a cab," I said and walked from the room, making sure to keep my stride steady and not look at them. I would not cry. I would not show emotion. I would just keep walking out.

When I got outside, I realised I was still wearing Eric's pyjamas. I couldn't go back in there, though. I shivered in the cold and wrapped my arms around myself to keep warm.

I heard someone approach me. My heart jumped. Maybe he'd come to apologise.

Jack thrust a bag at me.

"You left your clothes behind."

I took the bag and fished my big cardigan out, wrapping it around myself. It'd hide the elephant print on the pyjamas and keep me warm.

"You didn't have to run off."

"Well, I didn't feel very welcome, you know."

He cupped my face in his hand and looked into my eyes for a moment.

"Don't fall for me, Hannah. I'm not the kind of guy a princess like you should be thinking about. I'm damaged, more than you know. Women like Nancy know how to deal with me. But you, I'd destroy you without even meaning to."

I jerked my head away.

"What the hell are you talking about? I was having a fun time with Eric until the two of you came bursting in, so I have no idea what your stupid speech means. If anyone is falling for anyone here, I'd say *you* were falling for *me*. I'm not interested in you, not one little bit."

I glared at him through narrowed eyes.

"Yeah, well I'm not interested in you either." He folded his arms, practically snarling at me.

"Fine."

"Fine."

With that, the cab pulled up and I drove away.

Chapter 21

I punched the dashboard of the cab and screamed. The driver stole glances at me, thinking he had a crazy girl in his cab. Jack bloody infuriating Colt. I could kill him.

I'd given the cab driver my address but, when I got over my punching fit, I changed my mind. I'd still not heard back from Angie, so I searched in the bag for my phone. I pulled everything out of that bag, my manky old clothes and all, but I couldn't find that phone. I must've left it in Jack's bedroom, along with the dirty tissues. That gave me a small buzz, to think of all those tissues sitting around when he took that nasty woman to his bed.

I'd go to Angie's place and try to talk things over with her. When I explained, she'd be cool with everything, surely.

As if to make things worse, it started raining. I watched the drops splat on the window of the cab as the world outside refracted through them. The other day, when Jack had caressed my hair, I'd felt safe, like there was someone in this horrible world looking out for me, but now, once again, I felt alone. Who did I have? Not my father, obviously. Not Jack. Not Angie, unless I made things right with her. I'd had so many friends once. People practically begging me to hang out with them, to go to their parties, to date them. Even then, I'd known it meant nothing. I saw them turn on anyone who wore the wrong clothes or had the wrong haircut. I'd been the same. I didn't even think anything of cutting someone who'd committed a slight transgression. We were an exclusive club and you had to know the rules to belong or it wouldn't be exclusive any more, obviously. Now I'd become a university dropout with a very dubious income, a shitty room and maybe three decent outfits, sitting in a cab, trying not to drown in self-pity.

When the cab pulled up, I put my bag on my head to protect myself from the rain and ran to Angie's building.

"What do you want?" she asked when she answered the door. She stood with one hand on the door as though she'd pull it shut any minute.

"Can we talk?" I shivered. Even in that short distance, I'd managed to get damp in the rain.

"I don't think we have anything to talk about." She started to pull the door shut.

"Angie, is this about Jack? That was nothing. You got it all wrong."

She opened the door a crack.

"I got what wrong? I don't even know you, Hannah. I've worked my guts out helping you and I thought our agreement was that you'd help me with Jack. But, even more than that, I thought we were friends. I thought we were in this together. Now, I'm wondering if you were just using me. I don't really want to talk to you right now. And you owe me fifteen sixty-five for groceries."

She pulled the door shut and I stood staring at it, then knocked again. She had to talk. She had to let me explain. How could I make things right if she wouldn't talk me?

"Angie, open up." I banged on the door. "Angie! Angie! Talk to me. You are my friend, right?"

My only friend. I stopped knocking and listened for her. I could hear nothing, though. I knocked again.

"If it's about the money, you can have money. It's not important. Just let me in so we can talk."

I heard footsteps and grinned. We'd make up. She'd listen to me and see reason, then we'd be friends again and sit around bitching about what a bastard Jack was and making more plans for the band.

But the door didn't open. Instead, Angie turned on the stereo as loud as she could to drown me out.

I turned away. I'd really ruined things. The only person who still liked me was Eric, and I worried about his feelings for me. I didn't want to give him any false hope that things could be more than friendship between us.

I couldn't stay in Angie's doorway all night but I had no desire to go out into that rain again. It was only a few blocks to my place, so too close to even get a cab.

I ran out into the street and turned onto High Street, totally forgetting how crowded it got at night, with drunks crowding onto the streets outside cafés and bars to smoke. I'd have to run past them all unless I wanted to cut through one of the dimly lit back alleys. I figured it would be safer sticking to the main street. If I had to deal with drunks, better it should be in a busy well-lit street.

I huddled in a doorway and rolled up the legs of my PJ bottoms. They'd already gotten soaked and flapped against my legs in the most disturbingly gross manner. I looked like a drowned rat, a rat in elephant PJs.

I wrapped my cardigan tighter around myself and pulled my door keys out of the bag and held them in my hand, ready to run inside when I got home, then took off down the street.

"Whoa, baby, looking sexy!"

As I expected, shitty guys called out to me. I kept my head down and ran past them. Hopefully, they'd be too taken with their own drunken wit to worry about me. I just wanted to get home to my own room, where I could escape from this shitty world. I could lock the door behind myself and hide with the blankets over my head. Well, first I'd have a shower and put on some warm clothes. Maybe tomorrow everything would seem okay. Maybe this rain would wash the world clean and I wouldn't have to deal with creepy rock stars and oversensitive friends and weirdo drunks.

Another guy grabbed at me. I jerked away from him and sped on. This would have to be the most hellish night of my life. If Satan himself appeared and threatened to take me to the fiery depths of Hell, I'd welcome it.

As I waited to cross the sidestreet, a car pulled up, splashing water all over me. I shouldn't have expected anything less. I pretty much couldn't think of anything worse. My nose had started running again and I just wiped it on my sleeve. I was filthy anyway and I think I smeared dirt and grime over my face. My hair hung down in rat's tails and I could feel the rain dripping off my fringe, in cold rivulets down my face.

I ran along the next section of street. I just needed to get past there and I'd be home. It'd only be five minutes and I'd be in a warm shower.

As I ran by the last bar on the street, I barged into someone, like hitting a brick wall.

"Sorry, sorry," I said, preparing to run on, but he had hold of me.

He brought his face close to mine and scrutinised it.

"I know you. Hannah Sorrento." He stepped back and looked me up and down. "Hannah Sorrento, I can't believe it. You've come down in the world."

My heart stopped.

Then he laughed a lot and nudged his friend. I tried to walk off but they blocked my way. The pair of them were huge.

See, here's the thing. When I was in school, I wasn't always so nice. Sometimes, I might have been a bit mean. Only in fun, you know. But some people don't see it like that. Some people stew over those things and hold it against a person for life. Maybe even looking for revenge. I include Mitch and Cameron in those people. Big, gallomping farm boys with no brains but lots of simmering resentment.

Mitch leaned over right in my face.

"Hah, those rumours I heard about her father must be true. He's a swindler." He pushed me to Cameron.

"Karma's a bitch, isn't it, Hannah?"

There was another one in their group, too. Frog-face. I couldn't remember his real name. He'd always been known as Frog-face. He did something in the media now. As a camera flash went off in my face, blinding me for an instant, I remembered. He was a journalist.

Chapter 22

The next morning, I walked into the café with my head held high. So they'd taken a few photos. That didn't mean anything.

Then I saw it. The newspaper sitting on the table near the barista. A huge photo on the front page of a bedraggled girl. A pain shot through my heart. A sharp, horrible pain that radiated out all over my being.

I couldn't look at that picture. I didn't even recognise the person on the front of the paper. She looked filthy and poor and ugly. I turned the paper face down, hoping it would disappear, but it seemed like the noise and chatter in the café had turned up to deafening levels and the eyes of everyone in the room burned into my back.

After I gave my order, I turned to look for a seat. I took a few steps, then returned and picked up the paper. I had to read the story, even if it shattered me.

At least I looked presentable again. I'd put on my most expensive dress. An Alexander Wang woollen dress, casual but unmistakably designer. It was one of only three designer dresses I'd kept. Well, it'd been four, but that linen dress was never going to be wearable after the dryer incident. I'd paired it with a cashmere cardigan and a great pair of heels. I'd paid extra attention to my hair and make-up too, then surrounded myself with an aura of expensive perfume. No one would equate me with that bedraggled creature in the paper in the elephant pyjamas. I felt protected.

I wanted to buy up every copy of that paper and burn them all. Maybe run around the entire city and buy every copy and burn the lot. But that would cost a fortune, and what about the people who got their paper home delivered? I could never get rid of them all. No matter what I did, people would see that photo and they'd read those words.

Maybe if I dyed my hair and had plastic surgery, no one would ever recognise me. I needed a hat. A big hat that would cover my face.

I held my head high as I walked through the room. I defied anyone to judge me. But I found a corner table where I could keep my back to the room.

The pain in my heart kept twisting. All those years when Dad talked about never causing a scandal, never giving anyone reason to talk bad about us – that meant nothing now. The whole city would see our shame.

While I waited, I picked up the paper, by the edge as though it was dirty and would poison my skin. I didn't want to read the news story but I needed to know what they said about me. I picked away at it like a scab on my knee, reading a few words, then cringing too much to continue. I threw the paper face down on the table, not wanting that pathetic me staring up before I'd even had my coffee.

I slowly turned it over. God, I looked bad. I never imagined that, even on my worst day, I could look so bad. Maybe they'd Photoshopped the photo to add extra ugly to my face. There was the big photo of me looking startled, close up, with all the impact of the soaking wet hair and the dirty splattered face and the sodden pyjamas.

"Millionaire Family's Downfall," the headline read.

I imagined all those bitches I'd been at school with, the ones that hated me, reading this and laughing. I could almost hear their laughter ringing out over the city. Saying I deserved this, that they'd always known.

There was another smaller picture with my hand covering my face. They'd taken that one as I tried to get away. After they'd extracted every bit of humiliation and torture they could out of me, they let me run off. I'd had to take all sorts of jeers about Dad being a criminal and conman, though. They'd said he'd end up in jail if he was caught. That made me wonder if maybe I should've loaned him the money. Maybe, if I'd been a bit more sympathetic then, he'd have been able to save himself.

I wouldn't think about it. Thinking about it made my eyes prickle. I'd wait until I was alone in my room, then I could fall apart.

"Sheesh, what kinda trouble do you get yourself in without me around?"

Angie slid into the seat opposite me as though nothing had happened. I had half a mind to tell her to clear out. I didn't need her, especially after what she'd said last night. But, to be honest, I could've jumped up and kissed her. She was talking to me again, so something had to be right and good. Even if she was angry, angry and talking beat the hell out of angry and silent.

"You're not still mad?" I asked, and shot her a weak smile.

"I'm mad. I mean, you said you were too sick to work, then I get to your place and you're rolling around on the bed with Jack Colt. What's with that? But what's the point of being mad if you don't know I'm mad, so I thought I'd come here. Then I saw that picture on the front of the paper. You probably don't need more shit today, huh?"

"It was nothing. He was wiping my nose." It did sound a little bit wrong and unbelievable when I said it like that. I mean, who has some bad boy rock star in their bedroom, rolling around wiping snot? Like some kind of sicko fetish or something. No wonder he preferred the skanky chick. At least she wasn't snotty.

"Aha, you expect me to believe that?"

"Well, it's true." I grimaced at her and wiped my nose to prove my point.

"Wow, even when you're sick, your life is a huge drama. And now this whole exposé thing. What the hell is with you?"

She picked up the paper.

"It's like you're one of those celebrities that get embroiled in a scandal. Look at you, hand over your face. Did you try to smash the camera out of his hand? I'd have totally done that. Smashed it to the ground."

"I'm not *like* one of those celebrities. I am one. This is my life, Angie. The scandal and all that. Read it to me. I can't bear to read it myself. I really can't bear to look at that photo either."

Even though I laughed, I'd have nightmares about this for the rest of my life.

Angie picked up the paper.

"Twageeedy befalls one of zee country's reeechest—"

"Why are you reading like that? What's with the French accent?"

Angie set the paper down, grinning at me.

"I thought it'd be easier for you if I did it in a silly voice. Like it would take some of the pain out of it."

"You think there's going to be pain?"

She nodded her head. "You don't get a photo like that without pain. Hey, was your dad really one of the richest men in the country? No wonder you act so snotty some of the time. So, where's all the money?"

"Gone. It's all gone." I wanted to wrap myself in self-pity, but I couldn't with Angie beside me. She made me laugh and that took the edge off the pain.

"It says here he's planted some of it offshore."

There was money? Well, where was it? Dad sure as hell hadn't looked as if he had any. No one had mentioned any money, and I wasn't sure if it was one of those things the paper makes up or if it was true.

"They also say he was a swindler. He was involved in the underworld and all kinds of organised crime. Did you know that?"

I shook my head.

"Wow, they might end up making a movie about him. Who'd play you? Maybe Taylor Swift? And I could get someone hot to play me. Maybe I could play myself. That'd be really cool."

"I don't think it'd be cool at all." I sniffed again. "And I'd want Anne Hathaway, not Taylor Swift. Can Taylor Swift even act? But back to the story. This is my dad you're talking about, not some random person in the paper."

Angie scanned through the article.

"It doesn't say much else. Just all that about underworld connections. And that he's disappeared, and that you were the socialite daughter."

"Argghh, that's foul. Like I'm some airhead. I was at university and I was studying. It's not like I spent my entire time going to charity fundraisers and garden parties. I would've taken over the company if there was a company left to take over."

Angie turned the page on the paper.

"Who's Tom?"

"Tom! What about him?" A least Tom should have a good thing to say about me. "He's my boyfriend."

Angie raised her eyebrow in a way that spoke volumes.

"He says he never had a relationship with you. You were just casual acquaintances. And that he always thought there was something fishy going on." Angie folded the paper and threw it on the table. "Well, at least you don't have to feel guilty about fooling around with Jack now."

"I wasn't fooling... shut up, Angie. What a jerk. He should be here standing by my side, supporting me."

"Like Eric?"

"Huh?"

I turned around to see Eric walking through the café. He saw us and raised his eyebrows.

"I thought you'd be here if you weren't at home. I've got your phone."

He sat down with us and looked at the paper.

"I'm sure it's all lies and beat-up. The papers are full of shit. I don't believe a word of it."

"To be honest, I don't know what to believe." You'd think I'd have known if dodgy shit was going down, but I only saw the things Dad wanted me to see. There had never been any reason to mistrust him.

"You can believe in me," said Angie.

"And me too," said Eric. "I'll support you."

"Thanks, guys." Some warmth crept into my heart. I felt as if I could probably face the day. "I have to organise this record company meeting. If I do that, then maybe I can be successful enough in my own right that everyone forgets about this. I hope."

Eric reached over and grabbed my hand. I smiled at him. I could survive this. But really I wondered if it would be okay. They'd said Dad might go to jail. I didn't know if that was true, but he had gone into hiding. It wasn't a very good sign about the whole okay-ness of this.

My appetite had come back and I really wanted some French toast. Maybe with a side of bacon.

Eric left to meet a client but told me to call him if I needed anything.

Later, when the café was quiet, I rang the record company. I asked for the man who'd given me the card. The receptionist asked my name.

I could hear her suck in her breath when I said it. There was only the briefest of pauses, then she said she'd put me through.

I waited for a while, listening to the hold music. While I waited, I went over what I'd say in my head. I wanted to sound confident and self-assured. As if I did this kind of thing all the time and it meant nothing. As if we had heaps of offers on the table and I was working out which was the best. I could do that. I could be a hard-headed business bitch. Even if my palms were a little moist and the pulse at my temple throbbed.

The phone clicked. I was ready to go into action.

Before I could talk, though, the receptionist came back on the line.

"Sorry, he's in a meeting right now. I'll get him to call you back."

I gave her my details.

I put my phone on the table and waited for their call.

I spend most of the day at the café, working on plans for the band. We had a pretty full calendar now, with bookings most weekends for the next few months. Word had gotten around about their success at the Metropolis and it seemed so much easier to get them booked into decent places. I sent all the details to the music press and gave them to Angie for the website. I checked their Twitter and Facebook. Whoa, the number of followers kept climbing, but what some of those girls posted, it was just plain wrong. I did not need to see all those boobs and butts.

I thought about booking a tour. We could travel up the coast. I'd have to discuss it with the guys next time. And support gigs. We should try to get support gigs with some big-name bands.

My phone hadn't rung all day. I picked it up to check it was working properly.

"It's still early yet," said Angie. "They might call back soon."

Angie sat beside me most of the day, doodling ideas in a notebook.

"So, what do you think of Jack Colt?" she asked. "You haven't really said."

"I've told you. I'm not interested in him."

"Yeah, you say that, but you can't say it without blushing. You blush and you squirm like a schoolgirl. He's got you in your pants with his Jack Magic! I'm surprised you don't have his name written all over your notebook with hearts around it."

"You can't talk. You do have his name written in hearts in your notebook."

Angie laughed and looked down at her notebook.

"I don't like him, Angie, but I respond to him. You know, on a lustful level. Like, when he's around, my skin feels especially sensitive and my heart beats a little faster. I do stupid things and... I dunno. Maybe it's a lust thing. But I don't *like* him."

"Oh, you've got it bad. Maybe you should just screw him and get him out of your system."

"Maybe. Or maybe not. He was a total jerk the last time I saw him. There's something not right with him."

"There's a lot that *is* right. His butt, his shoulders, his eyes..."

"I mean in his head."

"I'd go there, regardless."

"Yeah, that's obvious. But he scares me sometimes."

I wondered if I should tell her about how he'd attacked me, but she jumped up to go to class. I figured I should leave too. A person couldn't spend all day stuck in a café. I felt a bit wired after three cups of coffee but I didn't feel nearly so stressed about the story in the paper. Who even pays that much attention to the papers anyway?

I paid up and left the café, wondering if I should go home and sleep. I still felt a bit sick and it hadn't helped getting caught in the rain.

"It's her!" I heard someone yell as I walked out the café door. Then a camera got thrust in my face.

I had no idea what was going on. Before I could get away, others had come to join him. They snapped photos and bombarded me with questions. I put my hands up to cover my face and didn't speak.

"Where's your father, Hannah?" one guy shouted at me, and soon the rest joined in.

"I don't know. I don't know."

I wrapped my arms around myself and tried to move through but they closed in tighter around me, like a pack of animals after my blood. I could feel the sheen of sweat on my forehead and my arms began to shake. I didn't know why they were doing this. I didn't know anything. I heard another shutter go off and flinched away from the sound.

My legs went weak, as though I'd buckle to the ground, but I could only think of being strong and not letting them see they were getting to me. Surely they'd go away. *You have to be stronger than anyone*, I heard my dad say.

"I haven't done anything wrong," I muttered under my breath. "I haven't done anything wrong."

But the questions kept coming. I didn't know what they were even talking about. Huge sobs rose up in my throat and I kept my head down, not wanting them to see.

Then one of them grabbed me.

"Come on, Hannah, give us a story."

Why did they keep saying my name as if they knew me? He clutched me tighter and I tried to shake him off, screaming at him to let me go.

Then someone broke through the crowd and took hold of me, dragging me away.

"Jack?"

He'd pulled the top of his hoodie over his head so they couldn't snap photos of him and pushed them aside with his body. A couple of them sized him up and then stepped aside. He grabbed me by the wrist and pulled me after him down the street.

"Don't stop. Keep walking and look calm. We'll go to my car and get you out of here."

"I don't know anything. I did nothing wrong. Why are they harassing me?"

"They just want a story. They don't care. If you say anything, it will be a quote for them. Did you say anything to them?"

"Nothing. Just to leave me alone. It's wrong. How can people just take pictures of you and put them in the paper without you even agreeing? I never gave them permission."

"They're the media. They can do what they want." Jack shrugged, and I wondered if he'd dealt with the media before.

We got to his car and he opened the doors.

"I'm glad to get out of there."

"Don't worry," he said, checking his rear-view mirror. "In a few days, it'll be something else. People don't have a very long attention span."

"I hope so."

Unless Dad got found – then it would happen again. Maybe it was better for him to stay hidden. Even if he'd gotten us into this mess, I didn't want him going to jail and having to deal with the harassment. I had to find out what was going on. I needed to know the full story instead of being a dumb airhead. Someone needed to fix this mess, and it looked as if that had to be me.

"Can you take me somewhere?" I asked.

He raised an eyebrow.

"Dad's lawyer. I need to talk to him."

Chapter 23

At first, Frank wouldn't tell me anything. He said it was better I didn't know, because then I couldn't let anything slip. That just made me realise that there might be more going on than I'd thought.

Jack had said he'd wait in the car outside Frank's house, but when Frank started talking, I realised maybe it would take longer than a few minutes.

Frank paced around his study, unable to settle. The whole room said successful lawyer, as though it were taken completely from an old-school lawyer movie set – the heavy wooden desk in the middle of the room that looked as if it'd been in the family for generations, the leather sofa that smelt of – well, leather, but also cigars and serious business decisions, the bookcase with leather-bound tomes of legal stuff. I sat on the sofa, playing with my bag, twisting the strap in my hands, as though that would make things any better.

I waited for Frank to speak but, after he'd offered me a drink and taken me into the study, he'd not said a word. The silence grew as solid and leathery as everything in the room.

"Where's my father?" I asked. "Is he in town or has he gone away?"

Frank looked at me as though assessing what he should say. He stood, leaning on the back of a chair. After a minute, it seemed as if he made a decision.

"He's in Asia. You can't tell anyone, though. And I can't tell you where."

"I think I know."

"Maybe you do," he replied, with a half-smile that seemed to confirm my suspicions. I had no idea who that man had been, though, or even what area he lived in. All I could remember was that market.

"Is there a warrant out for his arrest?" I asked. Surely, he'd not have put me in a position of harbouring a wanted criminal. I didn't want to get into this any deeper than I was, even though he was my father.

"No," said Frank. "He's under investigation, but they haven't found anything yet."

I twisted the strap of my bag tighter around my fingers. I wasn't sure how much of this I really did want to know, and I had to steel myself to hear the worst. This nightmare just got deeper and deeper.

"Is there anything to find?"

"Look, Hannah, there is stuff. It's not bad stuff. It's normal business practice, but it might not be entirely within the law. If they dig around enough, they will be able to find a few things to pin on him. It depends on how thorough they want to be. But, if they do that, a lot of dirt on a lot of people will come out. It's not just your dad involved in all this."

I sighed. It was all a mess. I didn't want to be in the middle of it. I'd never asked to be involved. They could take it all back – all the designer clothes and the fancy schools and the cars and the ponies. I'd much rather have a simple life, without the scandal and fuss. I'd been a princess, but maybe it hadn't been worth it if this was the price I had to pay. Maybe it would've been better to live in an ordinary house with an ordinary life.

"So, what should I do? I got swarmed by the press today. Can I sue them for defamation? Why do they keep after me when I don't know anything?"

Frank paced the floor again. I'd feel much better if he'd just settle down.

"I think you should lay low for a while. Keep out of the public eye."

"The public eye! I just went out for coffee. I should stop drinking coffee? Never leave my house?"

They knew the area I lived in. They knew where to find me. Soon enough, one of them would follow me and find out where I lived. Then they'd talk to the people in the building – none of them would have the sense to keep away from the press – and there'd be photos of my squalid living conditions all over the paper. And I'd never have a minute's peace from them all being there.

"It'd just be for a week or so, until it blows over."

"I can't go out for coffee for a week? What about the band? I'm their manager. I can't keep a low profile with that. I have to go out and do things. This is such a mess."

"It's only a week. Do you have any friends you could stay with?"

I thought about that. I could hardly stay with Jack and Eric, after what had happened the other night. I didn't want to be around Jack Colt when he brought chicks home with him. Plus, I couldn't ask him to sleep on the couch for the next week. Angie would let me stay, but her flat was so tiny. I'd be in the way and we'd get on each other's nerves, which I really didn't want since she just started talking to me again.

I shook my head.

"You could stay here. I'd put you up in the spare room. It'd be fine for a week or so."

This may seem really awful, since Frank had never actually done anything and always acted so nice to me, but he creeped me out. Even when I was a kid and I didn't know about creepy "uncles," I didn't like being alone with him. He'd never touched me. He'd never even suggested anything wrong, but there was something about him, a look in his eyes that I didn't trust. I'd much rather not stay with him. He'd already offered a few times before, but I'd refused.

"I don't want you get into any more trouble with us, Frank. I'll manage. Maybe I could move out of my flat. I only rent by the week and it's not like it's a very nice place, anyway. Since all the press know I'm around that area, I'll get right out of there."

He nodded in agreement.

"That's probably a good idea. Maybe take a week off. Go on holidays."

"I don't have enough money to go on holidays, and besides, I have manager work to do. We have some record company people interested in the band. I want to get onto that before the idea goes cold."

Frank sat down on the sofa beside me.

"Hannah, they were interested before. When it was just a band that looked like it could make the big time. They are no longer that. They are connected to the scandal. I don't know if they'll be such hot property now. Have you heard from the record company?"

I shook my head. "But they might just be busy?"

Frank shook his head slowly.

"People like that are never busy if they think they'll make money out of you. They will say they're too busy, though, until they work out if this is a good thing or not. None of them will have the guts to make a decision until this all plays out. Maybe you'll add a touch of infamy, maybe you'll be the kiss of death..."

I gulped. That was the last thing I wanted to hear. The band was all I had. My livelihood, my friends, my reason for getting out of bed in the morning were all tied up in that band. I didn't want to be the one to ruin it for everyone, but if I gave it all up, what would I do with my life?

"If you want to get away, I have a place down the coast. Maybe that's best, after all. It's very private, a nice beach right outside the door, and all the mod cons, including a coffee machine."

It made me angry that he offered now but hadn't said anything about a beach house when I moved into my crummy room. I'd known he got off on seeing me poor and hopeless.

He handed me an envelope with the keys and I put them in my bag without even thinking.

"There's a map in the envelope. I know the weather is bad at the moment, but you'd be out of all this and have time to think. Take a friend or two, it's a huge place. You might as well use it."

I nodded, still not convinced. How could I tell the guys about this? Of course, it made sense with Frank spelling it out like that.

"Hannah," he said as I was leaving. "At the moment, you are more of a liability than an asset to that band."

It was as though he could read my thoughts.

When I got back to the car, Jack was playing on his phone. I banged on the window and he jumped in fright.

"How'd you go?"

For a moment, I thought about telling him everything. Well, the bit about me being a liability to the band, anyway. I really did think about telling him, and usually I'm not a coward, but as I looked into his brown eyes, so full of concern, I couldn't say anything to sever this connection. I'd think about it and tell him later.

"He wants me to go to his place by the beach. He says it's pretty secluded but I'm not sure. Do I want to go to a secluded place down the coast? It could be really scary." Secluded means axe murderers can get you, and your body isn't even found for months.

"Sounds like paradise to me." Jack grinned and brushed his hair out of his face.

"You need a haircut," I said.

"What? Cut the famous Jack Colt hair? Have women all over this city fall into despondency? This hair is my fortune, babe. It's my ticket to panty town."

I slapped his arm. He could be so cheesy sometimes.

"Why don't you come with me?" I asked, without thinking about all that entailed. "Oh, that's probably not a good idea, right?"

"Why not?"

"You're busy and you don't want to be stuck in the middle of nowhere."

"No, no. It's perfect. We don't have any gigs until Saturday and I can drive back for that. And I've got some new songs I've been working on. Some peace and quiet at the beach is exactly what I need."

My heart skipped. I didn't know what I was feeling, though – anxiety or happiness or nervousness – or a volatile cocktail of them all. I mean, all alone in a shack in the middle of nowhere with Jack Colt? That had to be scary. What if he went nuts when we were there alone? But Eric had said it was only if he got disturbed in his sleep.

Still, what had happened to "don't fall in love with me, Hannah"?

"Maybe we could all go to the beach. Eric and Angie and, well, I guess even Spud." That'd be okay. There'd be a buffer zone. There'd be no shenanigans with all those people around.

"Good idea. But I think Eric has a big project on at the moment. We could ask him, but it wouldn't really be fair... he might feel obligated..."

I sighed. I guess I couldn't ask Angie to drop everything either.

We dropped by my place. Luckily, those reporters hadn't worked out where I lived yet. Because of the dodgy landlords, I had nothing in my name there. I paid rent in cash, I had no utilities connected and only had my mobile phone. I couldn't have picked a better place to live if I didn't want to be tracked down. I threw some clothes into a bag and got together some make-up and ended up back at the car in record time, just in case anyone was nosing around.

That went smoothly but then we got to Jack's place. I went in with him and waited for him to get his things together. He needed to pack his guitar and notebooks and everything he needed for songwriting. I sat on the couch and watched some daytime TV and didn't even notice Eric come in.

"Hey, Hannah, how's things?" he asked.

"I'm getting out of town. It's been too intense for me."

He smiled and sat on the couch beside me.

"Sounds like a plan. Anywhere in particular?"

"Yeah, heading down the coast to my uncle's beach house. Sounds like a good hiding spot."

Eric pulled out his phone and checked his messages.

"By the way, have you heard from the record company yet?"

My heart froze. I remembered Eric's support from this morning at the café. How he said he'd always stand by me. I should tell him the truth about the record company. I should let him know that I was destroying the band's future. But, yet again, the words wouldn't come out.

"Hey, I only called them today. Those guys must be all kinds of busy. I'll call them again tomorrow if I don't hear anything."

My voice sounded fake but Eric didn't seem to notice. He looked at me without making eye contact and started to say something but didn't finish. He was acting very weird.

He cleared his throat, but when I looked at him, he looked away.

I turned my focus back to the TV, to a story about a woman who became a hooker for Jesus. Was this stuff for real? To be honest, Eric didn't seem as if he had any project he was working on if he could sit around watching this stuff. Maybe I should've told him he could get back to work.

"Hannah," he said and I turned again.

He gazed down at his phone, not at me. I waited for him to talk.

"Hannah, I need to tell you something, it's kind of hard for me..."

"Hey, ready to go?" Jack had his guitar slung over his shoulder and a small bag in his hand. He called down from the landing.

Eric looked up at Jack and then at me.

"What were you going to say? We have to get going before dark."

I smiled at him encouragingly but he'd stood up. His eyes flashed darkly at me, almost as if he hated me. What had happened? All the muscles in his body had stiffened and he hovered over me like he wanted to speak, but then he just walked off.

I didn't want to hurt Eric, but I didn't have those kinds of feelings for him. I'd never met a sweeter guy or a better friend, but the only guy who could touch my heart was Jack Colt.

Chapter 24

"We should stop here and get some groceries," I said, seeing a supermarket up ahead. "I think this is the last big town before we get there."

Our drive down the coast had gone well. We'd missed most of the after-work commuters and had clear roads to drive on. Jack concentrated on his driving. He drove fast but not dangerously. I could relax with him behind the wheel. He didn't want to talk, but in an easy way, not the usual sulky not-talking way.

We pulled into the supermarket car park and went in to browse the aisles.

Inside the supermarket, country folk stood around chatting, getting in our way. When we passed them, they'd stop talking and look us up and down, silently judging, then return to their conversation. I guess we looked out of place. Jack in his black skinny jeans and studded leather jacket. His hair tied back in a ponytail and a chain of silver rings on his fingers. Me in a cute dress and heels, instead of sweatpants like everyone else.

I loaded up the trolley with tinned food and snacks.

"Can't you cook?" Jack asked, looking at the stuff I had.

"I can cook. It's just, we might have to store stuff for a while." I thought I was being really sensible.

"Right, because the place won't have a refrigerator and we can't drive to get more food."

"You never know. It's always good to be prepared for an emergency."

"I don't think any emergency requires eating canned chicken." He picked up the can and read the label. "Is this stuff even edible?"

"Wow, and *you* call *me* a princess!"

Jack grinned and put the canned chicken back on the shelf. Instead, he got vegetables and a huge tray of steaks.

"We don't need fourteen steaks."

"You mightn't. I'm a man."

"A caveman?"

He grinned. Sometimes, I wondered if he wasn't so far removed from a caveman. Except that he had that look in his eyes, the look that made girls practically swoon when he played guitar.

Jack grabbed some beer, so I got a couple of bottles of wine.

When we got back in the car, I turned the stereo down. It felt weird driving along without talking. He could damn well talk to me for a while.

"So, you're broke," he said, as he backed the car out of the car park.

"Way to state the obvious that is plastered all over the papers. I'm poor. Just like you." I sipped on a Coke. Maybe poorer, I thought.

"You aren't like me. You were raised like a princess. Even without money, you still have that. You can't change what's inside you."

"I can change," I said. If I thought about it, I already had. It'd only taken a few short months for me to become a different person, for the whole pattern of my life to change. I'd had no option but to change.

"If I was still at uni, I'd be taking exams now," I said. "I'd be so stressed. I guess this is a blessing in some ways. I get to relax and hang out at the beach instead."

He snorted.

"If you had the money, you'd go running back to that old life in an instant. You can't say you've changed when you never really had the choice. You still wear the designer clothes, even if you do eat canned chicken."

I didn't tell him how I'd sold my designer clothes to pay for the video or how I had to eat things I didn't need to cook so the smell didn't get into my clothes in my shitty room. Designer clothes are protection. They get you places you need to go. People judge you on how you dress. I didn't make the rules but I knew how to play by them. I'd taken damn good care of the few precious clothes I had left. If he thought that made me a bad person, then screw him.

"I'd sure as hell move out of that room if I had money, that's a fact. It's not like you're living in a hovel. You have it pretty damn sweet."

That must've been the wrong thing to say because he shut down after that. He turned up the music again as if to say *conversation over*. That made me mad. As if he was the one making all the rules and I didn't even know what they were. Things I could and couldn't say. Things I couldn't do. It's not as if it was my fault I was rich. It's just something you are born with, like being pretty or having good fashion sense.

I leaned against the window and stared out into the darkness, looking at the moon's reflection on the water and the lights of boats out to sea. Maybe being by the water would let me sort out all these emotions. Would I go running back to my old life? I wasn't so sure. I couldn't really go back, anyway. It seemed like a dream I'd had that had faded around the edges, and in the reality of day, I couldn't distinguish the facts. The things that had seemed important then, like hanging out with the right people and getting good grades and shopping, had come to mean nothing to me. As for Jack Colt, I think money meant more to him than he let on. He seemed to have some kind of hang-up about it, as if he was so much better for not having any.

We made good time getting to the beach town. The road had been clear and Jack drove well. Once we got to the town, I took out the map Frank had given me and navigated.

"You sure this is the right road?" asked Jack. "There doesn't seem to be much down here. And this road is wrecking the suspension on the car."

It was a pretty rough road but that was what the map said, the third turn-off after we left the town, then a couple of kilometres down the track to the beach house. The town itself had been tiny. A surf shop and a couple of souvenir shops and a café. Then there'd been a big stone pub on the corner, the old style with big verandahs. That'd pretty much been it.

"There's a place," I said. "Must be it. Pull over just here, there should be a turn-off."

In the lights of the car, it didn't look like much. Frank had said that it had all the mod cons, and I'd expected something closer to the beach, but this place was old and there was no beach in sight, as far as I could tell. Some of the boards were falling off the outside and the garden looked overgrown.

We grabbed our bags and headed to the front door.

"The key doesn't work," I said. I wriggled it, trying to get it into the lock. It didn't even fit, let alone turn.

"Let me try. You must be doing it wrong."

Jack took the key from me and tried to get into the lock. Not that he did any better.

"There's not another house?"

"This looks like it's the only one. Wouldn't it be on the map if we had to drive past another house? Maybe there's another door?"

We walked around the house, looking for another way in. I stumbled over a fishing net, left leaning against the side of the house. It was hard to see in the dark, trying to make my way through the long grass. The place had a strong smell of fish and a lot of weird stuff sitting around outside. Maybe Frank was into fishing.

"There's no other door. What should we do?" I asked, but there was no answer. "Jack? Jack?"

I walked back around to the front of the house, calling out to him. This was like a bad horror movie, where someone goes to investigate something and they never come back and then their body is found all dead and grotesque. I really hoped Jack hadn't been hacked up. I'd be all alone, and I'd have to fish the car keys out of his jeans' pocket and he'd probably be all blood-splattered and gross.

The front door of the house swung open. I screamed. It was the insane clown hacker dude, come to get me.

Jack stood in the doorway.

"What the hell are you doing? I thought you were the evil clown. Don't ever do that again." I beat my hands against his chest until he pushed me away.

"I got in through the window. This place is a little... rough... isn't it?"

I walked in and turned on the lights. He wasn't wrong. The floor was covered in worn lino and the walls were cheap chipboard. In some places, they weren't even lined. Frank had really talked this place up. The single room had mismatched furniture and the place was freezing cold. I couldn't even see a bathroom. There was more fishing stuff around the place – some fishing rods and nets. The whole place reeked of fish, too. Dead fish that had gone rotten in the sun.

"I'm famished," I said. I went into the kitchen area and freaked. "What's this?"

I stared at a big monster of a stove. It looked like something you'd see in a museum.

"I don't think we'll be cooking much, not unless you know something about historical stoves."

I pulled a bag of corn chips out of the bag of groceries and opened them.

"It looks like a wood oven. Is there any wood stacked anywhere?"

I found some in a basket near the stove. Jack mucked around and got a fire going, we just had to wait for it to heat up. He seemed to know exactly what he was doing. Arranging the wood in a pile over some newspaper. I'd have not even known where the fire should go.

I looked around some more.

"There is only one bed! What the hell?"

"That's okay," said Jack. "I'll take the sofa."

"The sofa is the bed." It didn't even look that comfortable, to be honest. It was about sixty years old and a couple of the springs looked as if they were busting through the worn fabric.

He didn't say anything, just wriggled his eyebrows.

"We can't share the sofa bed. We just can't." I'd rather sleep in the car.

"Why not? Do you think you can't control yourself around me?" He grinned. A wicked grin that signalled he had something in mind. His eyes locked into mine and did that thing that made me have no control over myself.

"Yeah, I can control myself. I can totally control myself." But my voice sounded strangled and unconvincing even to me.

With that, he walked over and stood within centimetres of me. Heat emanated from his body. He reached down and grabbed my wrists, the calloused skin of his fingers barely touching me. Chills ran from my wrists, through my body. I couldn't look at him. I didn't want him to see how much I wanted him, but he put his hand under my chin and raised my head. My heart raced so wildly, he must have been able to sense it. He stroked my cheek with a touch so light I could barely stand it. I didn't want to submit to him. I remembered how he'd been with that skanky chick. He did this all the time. It was just a game to him. But, at that moment, I wanted him to kiss me.

I gathered every bit of strength I had and tried to move away. I picked up my bag.

"I have to call Ang, let her know where I am."

That would give me some space. But he took my bag out of my hands.

"You can call her later."

And again, he moved toward me. His face so close to mine, it felt like the promise of a kiss. My hands trembled. I wanted to touch him. I wanted him to touch me. I couldn't even breathe. His hands moved down to circle my waist and he pressed his mouth to my neck. Suddenly, he nipped the skin. A soft nip that sent delicious shivers throughout my whole body.

I moved in closer, pressing myself against him. His hands ran down, tickling over my hips and then cupping my butt. His lips ran lines down my neck. I shivered all over.

He bit harder, making me moan. I gave a throaty laugh that didn't sound like my voice at all. This was what he did to me. He made me become someone else, and what I needed to decide was, did I like this Hannah? Did I want to be her?

I ran my hands along his chest, tracing his rock-hard muscles, moving down to feel every bump of every ab. I wanted to count each ridge along his stomach as though I were exploring the topography of an unknown land. I wanted to explore it with my fingers, my mouth, my tongue. I wanted to know the taste of him.

"Have you ever had a man make love to you, Hannah?" He ran his finger along my lips. "Make love to you so that you explode into a million little pieces and aren't quite sure how to put yourself back together again?"

I almost giggled, but the smouldering in his eyes stopped me. That look, it would burn a girl.

When his lips met mine, I turned to liquid. I melted into a mess of desire. My hands clutching for him, tangling in his hair and pulling him closer to me. No matter how hard he kissed me, it wasn't enough. The stubble of his chin scratched my face but I didn't care.

His hands inched up my thighs, under my dress. His fingers moved against my hot flesh and I had no desire to push them away. Even standing there in that horrible kitchen with its smell of rancid fat and fish guts, I'd let him touch me however he wanted.

"What's going on here?" a voice boomed from the doorway.

We both jumped apart like a couple of schoolkids being caught out.

"Marge, call the cops. There are a couple of randy kids broken in here."

I straightened my dress and turned to face him. An old guy glared at us. If he had a shotgun to hand, I reckon he would've shot us then and there. I could hear someone else, Marge, I guess, rustling around outside. The old guy had wild white hair sticking out of his beanie and a weathered face. He stared at us as if we were criminals.

"We didn't break in." Technically I guess we did. "Frank said we could use this place. He gave me the key."

"Frank? Frank Bolderwood?"

I nodded. This old man was starting to see some sense.

He snorted.

"Frank's place is down the next road. The third turn-off after the town. You kids don't have a lick of sense, do ya? As if Frank Bolderwood would have a dump like this. Couldn't ya tell by looking?"

"Well, I did think it was rather strange. We'll just get going, then..." I didn't want to look at Jack. He'd never let me hear the end of this. But I was sure we'd taken the third road after the town.

"Marge, no need for the cops. These kids are just fools. Leastways, they got the stove heated up for us." He turned to us. "Wanna stick around for dinner? Marge'll rustle you something up, quick smart."

I gulped. I didn't want to stick around with these people. I had a throbbing deep inside me and I needed to get away. I wanted Jack. I really wanted him. I needed to have him, right then and there. If we got to the real beach house, we could continue on from where we'd left off. Jack could ease the ache inside of me.

When we got in the car, though, I wished I'd taken them up on that invitation for dinner, since it'd have delayed the moment when we'd be alone together. I wanted him to touch me. I wanted to know what would've happened if we hadn't been interrupted. Even though I knew it was wrong. But Jack kept quiet, and the silence worried me.

Then I looked at him and saw the corners of his mouth twitch. He snorted out a laugh. I couldn't help myself either but started giggling too. Then, we both exploded with laughter.

"You were navigating. You said it was the third road. I hold you totally responsible."

"It was the third road. I counted. I can count to three, you know."

He just laughed some more. I wasn't going to win that one.

"Why do ridiculous things happen when you're around? You get me into a world of trouble. Every time I touch you, we get interrupted."

"Well, you were the one that broke in through the window. Maybe we should've realised then."

The key not fitting into the lock probably should've been a dead giveaway. If it didn't fit at the next place we found, I'd sleep in the car.

I tried to concentrate on finding the turn-off and not Jack's hands. His long fingers curled around the steering wheel. I could still feel the impression on my skin where he'd touched me. I wanted to keep that mood but I couldn't, not with him joking around like this.

"And what was with the clown thing? Were you getting scared on your own?"

"Shit, that's the road. Turn here."

Jack slammed on the brakes and turned down the road.

"Give me a bit more notice next time."

We drove for about five minutes, then saw a huge white house looming in front of us, perched up arrogantly, as if it had the right to command the entire seaside.

"Is that it? That's not a beach house. That's a mansion."

The place looked like something out of a design magazine, much more like I had expected. Definitely not a falling-down shack. We pulled up and parked the car in the garage under the house and took the stairs up to the front door. This time, the key fit in the lock. We walked inside and turned on the lights. This place was amazing, especially after my shitty flat. The whole interior was done out in red and white, with floor-to-ceiling windows looking out over the ocean, and a huge deck.

I carried the groceries into the kitchen. It had everything. Everything I ever needed. Including an awesome coffee machine. I squealed.

"What's up with you?"

"Coffee machine. And look at this kitchen. This is divine."

Jack stood by the kitchen table, laughing.

I grabbed some food out of the bags to start cooking dinner. The whole time, I watched Jack out of the corner of my eye, wondering if he intended to start back where he'd left off. Maybe he was glad that we'd been interrupted. I had no idea how he felt. One minute, he was all hot hands and kisses. The next minute, it was as if I didn't even exist. I couldn't read him. I couldn't tell if he just wanted to fool around and I was the only one handy or if it was something more. I didn't even know if I wanted anything more, I just knew that it thrilled me to be around him.

He didn't even look at me, just moved into the kitchen and started cooking up the steaks. He prepared some vegetables too. I hated to admit it, but he was better at cooking than me. I'd taken classes in exotic foods that needed a stack of ingredients and a whole day to prepare. I could make finger foods for parties, and exquisite cakes, but I could not prepare a simple meal like that. I watched him chopping and stirring, adding things to the pan and tasting.

After we ate dinner, it got a bit awkward. I looked over at Jack a few times to see if he was going to make a move, but he seemed engrossed in a movie on TV. It was almost as if he was purposely blocking me out, not wanting to look at me or talk to me or have any contact. Because he was like that, the silence grew and stretched between us. I couldn't work out how to bridge that gap.

I sat at one end of the couch and he sat at the other, a whole cushion between us. If I just moved over, got closer to him, maybe he'd react.

But how? How would he react? Would he welcome my advances or push me aside? He'd never had any problem showing me he wanted me before. How do people deal with that? Regular people? I'd been so used to men throwing themselves at me, I'd never learnt to make the first move.

Eventually, I said I was going to bed, trying to gauge how he'd respond.

"Night," he said, not taking his eyes off the TV.

I'd planned to give him a sultry look or even a toss of my head, but he'd ruined even that.

I climbed the stairs to the bedroom, hoping he'd come after me, but it was as if our embrace had just been a dream.

Waves crashing onto the beach outside and the low buzz of the television downstairs were the only noises. I sat on the edge of the bed, checking my phone, but my ears strained for the sound of his footsteps.

The record company hadn't called. I sent a text to Angie, then headed for my en suite bathroom and turned on the shower. I'd wash every thought of that guy away.

When I got into bed, though, I couldn't sleep. I had no idea what was going on in that man's stupid brain, how he could change from hot to cold so suddenly. I needed to figure him out.

I tossed and turned, replaying the grope at the crummy shack. It'd come from nowhere. And that time when we'd run away from the thug pool players. Each time, he'd not even built up to anything, just grabbed me. And I'd let him each time, as well. I'd not even tried to fight against him but willingly let him fondle me. I guess that let him think he could do what he wanted and get away with it.

How could he turn it on and off so easily?

I jumped out of bed and went downstairs. The movie must've finished and he was strumming away on his guitar. He finally looked up at me.

"What's going on?" I asked.

"Huh?"

"What's going on with you?" My heart pounded; I wasn't sure if I should push this, but I couldn't deal with the uncertainty. My voice came out thick and heavy, not light like I intended. "What's going on with us?"

He looked down at his guitar, moving his fingers along the frets but not making any sound.

"Do we have to talk about this now?"

I sat down.

"Yes. I need to know. Is this just a game to you? When you grab me and kiss me? Does it mean anything? I've got no idea what's going on."

I waited for him to reply, but he just strummed the guitar and ignored me. If he thought I'd give up, he could forget it. I knew he had a reputation for playing around, but I deserved an answer and he could bloody well give it to me. Finally, he turned to face me.

"Look, Hannah, I told you before. Don't get involved with me." He stared out the windows. I wanted to scream.

Yes, he'd told me, and I'd been more than willing to keep my distance, but it seemed like that distance just made him chase me more. Why did he touch me when he ended up pulling away? Was he purposely trying to torture me? I wanted to end this thing, one way or the other. I couldn't stand this roller coaster of emotions, not with everything else going on.

"Well, if that's the case, keep your hands to yourself. Don't start something you can't finish."

He turned to me. A slow grin spread across his face.

"Is that a challenge?" And that look came back into his eyes. In a moment, his hands would be on my body and his lips would be pressing against mine. He'd take me into his arms in a way I couldn't resist, and his scent would overwhelm me. He'd press against me and push me to respond. And I wanted that. I wanted that more than anything else in the world. Except I knew the price now, and I couldn't do this when I knew any moment he'd pull away and shut me out.

"It's not a challenge. It's a statement. Now, I'm going back to bed."

Chapter 25

I woke up the next morning to the smell of bacon sizzling. That made me really happy. For a few minutes. Then I realised. He was trying to win me over with bacon. No way would I fall for that scam. It'd been one thing to make a brave proclamation and storm out of the room, but a totally different thing to be in a cold bed all alone, knowing he was so close by. I had barely slept all night. And maybe, for a little while, I'd even let myself hope that he might knock on my door and talk to me and tell me that he was sorry and that he really did have feelings for me. I'd have forgiven him.

Instead I just had bad dreams. I pulled on a pair of jeans and a hoodie and rushed out of the house before he could talk to me. I headed for the beach. I couldn't cope with being alone in the house with him all day. We'd either end up in bed or killing each other. Maybe both.

As I walked, a strong wind blew along the beach. It whipped my hair around my face. I didn't care. I just put my head down and kept walking. The pounding of the waves onto the beach made me feel a little bit better. They were angry just like me. I didn't even know why I let him make me so mad. He was just a stupid guy who smelled good and played guitar good and looked good with his shirt off. That wasn't such a big thing.

I didn't even want to think about him, but I remembered how he'd saved me from those horrible reporters and how he'd looked after me when I was sick. Those weren't things guys did if they just wanted to play around, surely. He had to care just a little bit.

I picked up some pebbles from the beach and threw them into the sea. The spray from the ocean blew into my face, all salty and strong. I picked up more pebbles. Maybe if I threw every single pebble on this beach back into the sea, by then I wouldn't be angry any more. I threw the next one with more force. Seagulls squawked around me as if they were my own personal cheer squad.

I threw the next one even farther. I thought about hurling those rocks right at Jack Colt. That would feel good. I'd throw rocks at him and smash him up.

I held the last rock in my hand. It didn't help. All this throwing of rocks just made me feel tired, but the pain inside didn't get any smaller. I'd have to throw forever for that. I collapsed down into a squat and hugged my knees. Maybe I could stay there until I got blown away myself. I could float in the wind out over the sea and never come back or have to deal with any of this. I'd not have to be strong.

What had I expected? He fooled around with me but that was it. It's not as if it was ever going to be a happily-ever-after with him. Two-week limit, Angie had said. I didn't want a cheap shag and to pretend nothing happened the next day. That'd be awful and uncomfortable. I had to work with these guys. But there was no picture I could imagine in which Jack Colt and I had anything together.

We could be friends. That's it. That would be safe and sure. If I wanted to keep being their manager, that's what I needed to do. If I kept being their manager...

But the ache in my heart said something else. Something I didn't want to listen to. A pathetically lame part of my heart wanted to make a picture that included Jack Colt and me with hearts and flowers and happily-ever-afters. I'd pushed down that part of my heart ever since I'd met him, but it just wouldn't die. That part of my heart wanted him to take me in his arms and say "I love you," and that part of my heart wanted to say it back. But that would never happen.

Eventually, I got up. My fingers felt so frozen, I thought they'd snap off if I bent them, and the wind had burnt my face. And I really needed to pee.

I walked back to the house, not wanting to face Jack. Knowing at any minute, he'd turn on that chilling silence and make me feel as if I was nothing. I couldn't let him do that to me again. I had to stop this now, kill the last bit of hope and desire inside myself. While I still had that, he could break me at any time.

As I walked, I filled myself with resolve. I'd be stronger and tougher. I'd keep my distance from him and never let him toy with me again. I'd call Eric to come and pick me up or walk out to the main road and hitch a ride back to the city. Anything to avoid Jack Colt. The pressing need of my bladder pushed me on, growing more urgent the closer I got to the house. I raced up the steps to the front door and paused only to take off my shoes and tap out the sand.

"Hannah?" Jack called.

"Not now," I yelled, rushing up the stairs to the bathroom. Nothing he had to say was more vital than that.

And finally, relief.

When I finished, I waited in the bathroom, not wanting to go out and confront him. I didn't want to fight. I didn't want to talk. I just wanted to become numb and not have my stupid heart jumping all over the place with his moods.

"Hannah?" he asked again, as I walked back downstairs. He looked at me, and all my resolve melted. Somehow, he could do that to me. The hurt look buried deep in his eyes made me want to comfort him, when he should be comforting me. He stood at the foot of the stairs waiting.

He took my hand and pulled me to the sofa. I sat down beside him.

"I'm sorry," he said. Just like I'd wanted the night before. "I'm not good with this kind of thing. It's not that I don't like you, it's just that I'm not good..."

I looked at him, wondering why he thought that. Who was good at this kind of thing? Not me. I hated it but I needed to know how he felt.

"If I let you get too close, I might destroy you. I worry about that."

I nodded.

"I can survive. I've survived so far. Why don't you take a chance, Jack? Let me look after myself."

He pulled me into his arms and I rested my head on his chest. He didn't try to kiss me, he just caressed my hair and leaned his head on mine. I could hear the beating of his heart. I felt at peace in his arms. I reached over and took his other hand in mine. I traced along the outlines of his fingers. He had the most amazing hands of any man I'd met, so strong and yet so tender.

A lock of his hair swept down into his face and I brushed it back behind his ear. He took hold of my hand again, as though he couldn't bear to not hold it.

At that moment, without words, I knew he cared. Everything about him said so – his breath, his heartbeat, his touch. The feel of his hands brushing through my hair as though I was the only one in the world for him.

"Stay with me," he whispered.

I nodded. I felt safe here with him to protect me from the world. He pulled me closer to him. I didn't want to speak, I didn't want to move, scared that anything I did would break this moment between us. It had felt like every time we'd gotten close, something had come along to destroy that closeness. Finally, we could show our true feelings.

With his thumb, he stroked the palm of my hand.

"Don't you want to eat something?" he asked.

I shook my head. I did, but not right then. Soon, we'd have to get up and cook something to eat and we'd have to leave the beach in a few days but I didn't want to think about anything but that moment. I'd never dreamed I could feel that happiness.

We watched the wind blowing up a storm outside, but in here, we were warm and happy and protected.

Chapter 26

Of course, we couldn't stay in each other's arms, curled up like a pair of kittens, for long. While my heart was happy, there were other parts of me demanding attention. Before long, my hand ran up his chest, feeling the outline of the hard muscles. His fingers traced my cheek and our mouths sought each other. At first, his lips brushed lightly against mine, as though neither of us felt any rush, not through lack of desire but with the knowledge that we had forever.

He pulled away, uttering my name. He brushed back my hair and ran his finger over my lips. I playfully nipped at it.

Then my phone rang.

"Ignore it," he said.

He pressed hard against me, defying me to let it ring.

"I can't," I said. "It could be news about Dad."

He nodded, the realisation coming into his eyes that I would have to take it. If anything urgent had happened, I'd need to know straight away.

"Yes?" I answered, then listened to the explanation, waving at Jack to get me a pen and paper. "Yes, that sounds doable. It will take some juggling but we can rearrange our schedule for you."

I took the pen and wrote down the details, then hung up.

Looking at Jack, I took a deep breath. "Looks like we have to go back to the city."

"Bad news?"

"Not at all. The best. That was the TV station. They've had a band pull out of the line-up for *Rock! Live!* tonight and they need someone to fill in at the last moment. We'll need to leave at once. This is too hot to pass up."

Jack got it at once. He jumped up and threw some things in a bag. I wondered if I should've ignored the call. Would we ever get back to that place? Would he ever take me in his arms again? Maybe that once-in-a-lifetime moment had been ruined.

He noticed me staring out to sea and took my face in his hands.

"Don't worry," he said. "As soon as the show's over, we can head straight back here. We'll turn off our phones and be so far away from anyone that no one will touch us. Hours and hours of uninterrupted time."

The look in his eyes let me know he was thinking what I was thinking.

"You don't need to come with me, you know. If you are worried there's going to be trouble or any of that, we should be able to manage on our own. You can relax here."

"As if I'd miss this."

I rushed upstairs to shower and get changed. I need to look fantastic as the manager. We jumped in the car and headed off. I called Eric and Spud and let them know to meet us with the gear. Then I called Angie.

When she finished squealing, I asked her to bring me a change of clothes and meet us at the studio. We had to be there for setup at five, then for live recording at eight.

"I've got to record this. It's going to be huge. Oh, can I be in the audience? Get Jack to play near me so I can be on the telly. This is totes amayonnaising! I've always wanted to be in the audience. Oh, my dream is coming true."

When I hung up, Jack laughed at me.

"You need a change of clothes?"

"Yes, I didn't pack appropriately for this. I just wish I'd left a key to my place with Angie. Still, I'm sure she'll bring something decent for me to wear. Better than jeans."

"You are not actually going to be on TV yourself, you know. And I happen to like you in jeans."

"Oh, you do, do you? Well, that's nice. I'll take that into consideration when I'm getting dressed next time." I poked my tongue out at him.

"Yeah, you don't strike me as a chick who dresses to please her boyfriend."

I didn't say anything out loud. I didn't question what he'd said. I just took the word "boyfriend" and hugged it to my heart secretly, putting it away to pull out when I needed to be reassured.

"What are you grinning at?" he asked.

"Nothing. Nothing at all."

Eric, Spud and Angie were waiting in the car park at the studio.

"Okay, we have everything loaded up. We have to go in. The PA has some stuff to go over with us before rehearsal, releases to sign, all that kind of thing."

Eric seemed to be on top of it all. I nodded.

We walked down a corridor with pictures of stars framed on the walls.

I grabbed the bag off Angie and ran into the bathroom. I'd spilt a drink on myself in the car and my top felt gross and sticky.

I washed myself down and pulled the clothes out of the bag.

I wasn't sure what she was thinking, but the outfit Angie had packed so wasn't me. Still, I needed to change my top at least. I pulled out a tight black t-shirt and threw it on. It showed every curve of my torso. It looked almost indecent with the way it clung to me. Then, I pulled out a skirt and a pair of ripped tights. When I'd said I wanted a change, I meant to look *more* sophisticated, not like a band moll.

I kept my jeans on with the t-shirt. I tried to pull the hem of the tee down so it covered my flesh, but it just bounced back up again.

As I walked out, a girl with frizzy blond hair rushed up to us.

"Which of you are the band?" she asked.

"They are, and I'm the manager," I replied.

Jack turned around to look at me, his tongue almost hanging out.

As we followed the blonde, he slid his hand into my back pocket.

"Love the new look," he whispered in my ear.

"You three, get to make-up. I'll go over everything with your manager."

As they ran through the song, sounding pretty damn good in my opinion, I chatted to the blonde girl, who was the PA for the show. She seemed pretty into Spud, surprisingly enough.

"Sure, Jack's the good-looking one in the band, but he's a bit too pretty, you know?"

"Huh?" I'd never have used "pretty" to describe him.

"I mean, he's got those long eyelashes and that pouty mouth. Even though he looks rough and ready on the surface, I bet he's full of angst."

Yep, looked like she'd pretty well summed him up.

"Are you two an item?"

Who even says that? Was she like fifty years old?

I didn't answer but I felt my cheeks burn. Still, if I was going to announce our item-ness, it would not be to this chick.

"Spud's got a real ruggedness to him, though. You can see from that wild look in his eyes."

"He's got a girlfriend."

The blonde shrugged like she didn't care about that kind of thing.

Even though it was only a rehearsal, Jack strutted around the stage as if he owned the place. That was him – I could imagine that even if he played for an audience of two people, he'd still be a rock star onstage. I couldn't imagine that, not so long ago, I'd thought this was just wailing noise. This man, his words and the way he sang them, he could be someone amazing. He *was* someone amazing; it just needed the rest of the world to discover that.

And right now, there was only one obstacle in the way. I wrapped my arms around myself, my lips quivering. Could I be that obstacle? I was the first to admit, I could be a little selfish. I'd never really had to consider someone else's needs before. But could I let my selfish needs stand in his way of the band's success?

I still felt the warmth of Jack's embrace on my skin, but how long would those feelings last? If I told him the truth, he'd have no reason to see me, but if I didn't tell him... I imagined a fury that would shake the ground and cause buildings to collapse.

Then, there was the whole money issue. If I walked away from the band, I might well be poor for the rest of my life. I had no backup plan. If I walked away and they hit the big time, it'd be like walking away from a fortune. But then, it was a fortune they could only make without me.

The spotlight shone on Jack Colt. It emphasised his cheekbones and his pouty bottom lip. It emphasised the tousle of his hair. It emphasised the strength of his body. That spotlight shone as if it'd been created for the sole purpose of shining on Jack Colt.

We all went to the green room after rehearsal. The PA brought in some beers and a platter of food.

"Where's Spud?" I asked. I hadn't seen him since rehearsal.

Jack shrugged, grabbing another sandwich.

"He's around. He's the sucker, missing out on this food. These sandwiches are the best sandwiches in the history of sandwichdom."

He grinned at me, that look coming back into his eyes. I'd have been the happiest girl in the world at that moment if I could have returned that grin wholeheartedly.

I grabbed Angie's hand and asked her to go to the bathroom with me. I couldn't be this selfish person. I couldn't be the obstacle.

I told Angie my plan.

"Huh? No way?" Angie said. "You've done nothing but help the band. Why would anyone care what your dad has done?"

I shrugged. That's how life goes. Whether it was right or wrong, you couldn't fight it.

"I can't manage the band..."

"Yeah, you can. You totally can. It's not like I know what I'm doing. I just make it up as I go along."

I looked at her reflection in the bathroom mirror. I'd thought she was a freak when I first met her, but now this person standing beside me was my closest friend in the whole world.

She put her hand over mine.

"I'll do it, but only until this mess is cleared up. Then I'm handing it all back to you."

I shook my head.

"No, it can't work like that. I have to have nothing to do with the band at all. My name has to be totally unassociated with the whole thing."

She sighed. Then she smiled.

"Can I make them wear maid costumes and serve me cups of tea?"

I managed a weak grin.

"You'll have to take that up with them."

When an assistant called out that it was ten minutes to airtime, Angie slipped out of the bathroom. I needed a minute to sort myself out.

I fixed my hair in the mirror. I needed my hair done, but I sure as hell couldn't afford that. I didn't even recognise myself any more.

I opened the door but heard voices and closed it again. Angie had promised not to mention anything to the band, and I didn't want to tell them before they went on air. I wanted them calm and focused.

"Hey, Jack, I've got to talk to you. It's pretty urgent." That was Spud. Maybe he'd forgotten his lucky drumstick again.

I opened the door a crack.

"Melanie told me something..."

"Who's Melanie?" asked Jack.

"The PA. Blonde girl, great hooters... anyway, she reckons we're never going to get signed with Hannah as our manager. Hannah is deathly poison."

Jack laughed. As well he should. He believed in me. I knew it. I let out the breath I hadn't even realised I was holding.

"No kidding, mate. With all this scandal around her, and her old man, no one wants to touch her. Would you? That kind of shit is a killer. Melanie says they had a huge meeting before the show and it was a dead cert they weren't going to have us on. Because of *her*. You've got to get it, mate. She's a sinking ship and we've got to be the rats. We'd have been first pick otherwise, but this way, they called five other bands before us."

I waited for Jack to answer. For him to tell Spud it was a pack of lies and it didn't matter anyway. He'd stand by me. I opened the door even more so I could see his face and how he reacted.

Still, Jack didn't answer.

I sunk against the wall, waiting for Jack's response. I should've told him before. I should've told him in my own words instead of letting him hear all this nastiness from Spud and that backstabbing Melanie.

My jelly legs wouldn't move, even if I wanted to get out of the bathroom. I had to hold on to the wall just to stay upright. I needed to hear Jack say it was all right. I curled my hands, pinching my nails into the flesh of my palms, condensing my pain into that one place.

"Come on, mate. You want to dump her too. It's not like you give a rat's arse about her. You were the one who made the bet about buttering her up so we wouldn't have to deal with her stupid. 'We don't want no rich bitch playing at managing us,' that's what you said. 'She'll be eating out of my hand in no time, then we'll just do what we want.' I had respect for you when you said that, mate. Come on, have you boned her yet?"

Had Jack said that? Had he really? It made sense now. I gagged from the bile rising in my throat. Something hard and heavy pressed against my chest. I had to get out of this bathroom before I fainted. I had to get away.

I pushed the door open and marched down the corridor. Jack grabbed my arm as I walked past.

"Hannah," he called. "Hannah, let me explain—"

I shook him off. I'd heard enough of his lies. Tears prickled at my eyes but I scrunched my face to stop them falling. I wouldn't cry and I wouldn't turn back. I'd just keep walking. I had nothing. I was a joke. *You have to be stronger than anyone.* But why did I have to be strong? What was there to be strong for?

"Have you boned her yet?" Those words rang in my ears. No, but he came damn close. And he would've shared every last detail with Spud. The two of them laughing over how Jack had fooled me. All the caring words, all the soft touches were part of his game.

Even Angie – without the band to sweeten the deal, would she still be my friend? It'd never been me, not with anyone. It'd been what I had: money, the band.

"Five minutes to airtime. Get ready."

As I strode through the studio car park, I could hear him calling to me.

"Hannah, come back." His footsteps advanced on me and then they stopped.

"Jack, it's time to go on," Eric called. "Hurry up."

He'd go back. He'd disappear into the building because the one thing he cared about in this life was his band. More than he cared about me, more than he cared about himself, even. He'd get on that stage and play and forget that he even knew me or that he'd destroyed my life. I kept walking through the car park. I'd walk to the train station and go home and pack my bags. Then where? The beach house was no good any more. I couldn't stay with Angie and I had nowhere else to go. But I'd been left with nothing before and had survived. I'd survive again. I'd go somewhere else and get a job. Work in a bar or something. And I'd never see bloody Jack Colt again.

I got to the train station with a couple of minutes to spare before the next train. I paced the platform, torn between wanting to go back and punch Jack Colt in the face and wanting to get far, far away. I couldn't go back. If he tried to explain, if he sweet-talked me, would I handle it? Would I believe his words because I wanted to? Far better to put as much distance as possible between me and Jack Colt.

My phone beeped. Bloody Jack Colt. He had nothing to say that I wanted to hear. You can't just say sorry about something like that. When had he made the deal anyway? Right at the beginning after that first gig? Or when I'd been drunk and vomiting? That would explain the kiss on the forehead. Or was it later?

Then it hit me. That day we'd made the video, how he'd changed from snarly to nice, and had taken me drinking. How he'd saved my life. Or had he? Maybe that was a trick too.

When I looked at the display, though, it wasn't Jack. It was Dad. I gulped back my tears. Of course, it wasn't Jack. He'd be on camera right now. He'd be working his magic and turning on that charm. Breaking more hearts, but none of them broken more than mine. When he was on, he'd have forgotten he ever knew a girl called Hannah.

Up there, with the cameras on him, Jack would sparkle. They'd be sensational. Every girl, every woman, would want a piece of Jack Colt. This one appearance could make all his dreams come true.

"Have found a way to save the business, meet me here at once." That's what Dad's message said.

No more details than that but I assumed "here" was Thailand.

My tears fell heavily now. I could barely see to type out my reply. I'd be there. I'd be there on the next plane. Then Jack and Spud could laugh over me all they wanted. I wouldn't know. I'd be on a tropical beach sipping a cocktail out of a pineapple. I tried to smile but my mouth wouldn't go up at the corners. A woman sitting on a bench nearby pulled her child closer to her.

I pressed "send" on my reply as the train pulled into the station. The cameras would be swinging to Jack at this very moment. By the time I got home, he'd be offstage and on such a high. He might look for me but probably not, and then he'd go out drinking with the others and they could laugh about the way he'd played me big time. Stupid Hannah, too dumb to notice. A bit of pretty talk and a few kisses, that's all it'd taken. Too easy. He might even pick up another chick, like that one he'd had at the flat, and take her home. I was well out of there.

The train doors opened. As I stepped into the carriage, someone grabbed me. I struggled. Another reporter?

I'd had enough of bloody reporters just looking for someone else's misery to splash all over their front pages.

"Fuck off. No photos."

I swung around, prepared to hit him. I'd knock his camera to the ground before any more photos of me could appear on their front pages. As my fist connected with his face, I realised it wasn't a reporter.

It was Jack Colt.

THE END

Did you love *Bad Boy Rock Star*? Then you should read *Bad Boy vs Millionaire* by Candy J Starr!

When fate forced Hannah Sorrento to take on the management of indie rockers, Storm, she managed to survive but, when she found out she'd been played by their mercurial front man, Jack Colt, the betrayal hit her hard.

She flees to Tokyo, where her father orchestrates a deal to save their collapsed financial empire. A deal that involves a gorgeous millionaire.

Tamaki is everything Jack isn't and, with their similar backgrounds, he and Hannah form a bond. He offers her safety and security as well as a return to her luxurious lifestyle. But the passion Jack arouses in Hannah won't be denied.

In the sequel to Bad Boy Rock Star, can Hannah forgive Jack or will she take the sanctuary Tamaki offers?

Read more at candyjstarr.com.

Also by Candy J Starr

Access All Areas
Too Many Rock Stars

Bad Boy Rock Star
Bad Boy Rock Star
Bad Boy vs Millionaire
Bad Boy Redemption
Angie: A Short Story from the Bad Boy Rock Star Series
Bad Boy Rock Star: The Complete Story

Fallen Star
Rock You
Cry for You
Be With You

Standalone
Hands Off! The 100 Day Agreement

Watch for more at candyjstarr.com.

About the Author

Join the Candy J. Starr newsletter for good times, new release news and giveaways. Once your details are confirmed, I'll let you know how to get a copy of *Angie: A Short Short from the Bad Boy Rock Star series* for absolutely free as a special thank you. - http://candyjstarr.com/bad-boy-rock-star-mailing-list/

Candy J. Starr used to be a band manager until she realised that the band she managed was so lacking in charisma that they actually sucked the charisma out of any room they played. "Screw you," she said, leaving them to wallow in obscurity – totally forgetting that they owed her big bucks for video equipment hire.

Candy has filmed and interviewed some big names in the rock business, and a lot of small ones. She's seen the dirty little secrets that go on in the back rooms of band venues. She's seen the ugly side of rock and the very pretty one.

But, of course, everything she writes is fiction.

Thanks for buying and reading this book. If you enjoyed it, I'd totally love it if you took the time to leave a review.

Read more at candyjstarr.com.

Made in the USA
Coppell, TX
25 August 2022

82061186R10132